What the Hatmaker Heard

Books by Sandra Bretting

MURDER AT MORNINGSIDE

SOMETHING FOUL AT SWEETWATER

SOMEONE'S MAD AT THE HATTER

DEATH COMES TO DOGWOOD MANOR

ALL HATS ON DECK

WHAT THE HATMAKER HEARD

Published by Kensington Publishing Corporation

What the Hatmaker Heard

Sandra Bretting

LYRICAL UNDERGROUND
Kensington Publishing Corp.
www.kensingtonbooks.com

LYRICAL UNDERGROUND BOOKS are published by

Kensington Publishing Corp.
119 West 40th Street
New York, NY 10018

All Kensington titles, imprints, and distributed lines are available at special quantity discounts for bulk purchases for sales promotion, premiums, fund-raising, educational, or institutional use.

Special book excerpts or customized printings can also be created to fit specific needs. For details, write or phone the office of the Kensington Sales Manager: Kensington Publishing Corp., 119 West 40th Street, New York, NY 10018. Attn. Sales Department. Phone: 1-800-221-2647.

Lyrical Underground and Lyrical Underground logo Reg. US Pat. & TM Off.

First Electronic Edition: July 2020
ISBN-13: 978-1-5161-0576-2 (ebook)
ISBN-10: 1-5161-0576-1 (ebook)

First Print Edition: July 2020
ISBN-13: 978-1-5161-0579-3
ISBN-10: 1-5161-0579-6

Printed in the United States of America

Chapter 1

Like the exotic animals that boarded Noah's Ark so long ago, each architectural detail on the beautiful mansion in front of me had a perfectly matched mate to go with it.

First up was a pair of elegant mullioned windows, which flanked the front door like boxy lapels on a gentleman's dinner jacket. Next came a sweeping staircase, split in two, with the halves trailing to the ground like loose ends of a silk bowtie.

Finally, two spiraling water towers bookended the mansion, ready to catch whatever rainwater was lucky enough to fall on such a gorgeous property.

I stared at the house for a good minute or so, transfixed by the intricate details, the grand scale, and the unusual color choices made by the owner.

Whoever came up with the home's design outdid herself when it came to the paint. A limewash of pale yellow covered the stucco walls, while the shutters and banisters popped in a coat of peacock blue. Peacock blue! Such an inspired choice for the gingerbread style, and it made the white staircase even more striking.

I couldn't help but smile. Not because I loved jewel-tone colors and architectural symmetry, but because the mansion was so gloriously out of place. Here I'd driven past sugarcane field after sugarcane field, all of the ground parched by the July heat, only to find a bright Easter egg of a building nestled among the marshlands.

"There you are. I've been looking all over creation for you."

Lorelei Honeycutt, heiress to the property and my newest client at Crowning Glory, a hat shop I operated on the Great River Road, sidled up next to me. Not quite twenty-one, Lorelei possessed the creamy complexion of someone raised in the South—thank goodness the humidity was good for *something*—and she swallowed the tail end of her words, like every other Cajun who lived in this part of Louisiana.

"You found me." I smiled again, pleased to see my client looking so relaxed on the day before her wedding.

"I wanted to talk to you about the veil you made for me."

"Of course." I pointed to a nearby gazebo, which was disappointingly painted white. Why in the world would someone create an Easter egg in the marshlands and then plunk an ordinary gazebo next to it? It didn't make sense to me, and it made me appreciate the quirky mansion all the more.

But no matter, the gazebo still offered shade from the relentless sun and a chance to put up our feet while we spoke.

"Why don't we move into the shade?" I nodded to the gazebo. "It's hotter than a billy goat with a blowtorch out here."

"Fair enough." Lorelei took the lead and we headed for the lattice-trimmed gazebo.

"Now, you were saying something about your veil?" I smoothed a strand of auburn hair behind my ear, and my gaze automatically drifted south to the starburst of light on Lorelei's ring finger. Since I worked around brides every day, I'd grown accustomed to seeing some incredible engagement rings, but none could compare with the five-carat rock that graced Lorelei's left hand. It made my own one-carat diamond look like a pebble in comparison, but I wasn't one to complain.

"I'm a little nervous about the veil's girth, to be honest," Lorelei said. "Do y'all think it will fit going down the aisle?"

"Why, bless your heart. I can see why you might worry." While I normally saved "bless your hearts" for people who behaved badly, it seemed a fitting exclamation in this case. Like every first-time bride, Lorelei wanted to control a situation she didn't know much about. Having never planned a wedding before, she had no idea what was feasible and what wasn't.

"Anyway, a cathedral-length train can be intimidating if you're not used to wearing one. Especially one with three tiers. To make it less bulky, I'll cinch the fabric and bustle it beneath your bodice. That way it won't overwhelm you when you walk down the aisle. Afterward, I'll release it for the pictures."

"So, that's how you do it." Lorelei breathed a huge sigh of relief, obviously satisfied with my answer. "I don't want to look like a giant marshmallow walking down the aisle."

"I don't want you to either. And you won't. Trust me. It's all in the underpinning."

"Just in case…" Lorelei gazed at me hopefully, which was a look I'd come to recognize. She was about to ask me for a favor, and my answer would determine her everlasting happiness. Or that was what it probably felt like to her. "Do you think you could come to the rehearsal tonight? I know you're going to the ceremony tomorrow, but it'd really help me if you could be there tonight, too. I want to practice walking with the veil on."

"I don't see why not." Luckily, it was one of the more benign requests I'd received from a client. Very unlike the bride who asked me to remake her entire veil the week before her wedding, or the bride who changed her order from a cathedral-length veil to a perky fascinator faster than you could say, "Las Vegas elopement," or the bride who tried to compete with Princess Diana of England by ordering a forty-foot train, when her chapel's aisle only stretched twenty-five feet. *Gracious light.* Compared to those requests, Lorelei's question seemed downright tame.

Plus, I didn't have any plans tonight to speak of. Since we were right in the middle of the wedding season, most of my friends were hard at work. By now, Bo—my fiancé, Ambrose Jackson—would be up to his eyeballs in white tulle, Swarovski crystals, and dress patterns.

Bo owned a design studio next to mine, only he created couture wedding gowns that sold for thousands of dollars apiece. Thank goodness his hefty design fee silenced the naysayers, because many people originally sniffed at his "unmanly" occupation. As if someone should be faulted for following a dream, like Bo did. As far as I was concerned, my fiancé was the most manly-man I knew, and I didn't care one whit whether he designed ballgowns or plowed under a sugarcane field in a John Deere tractor. "Of course I can go to your rehearsal tonight. I don't have any plans, so it'd be no problem."

Lorelei exhaled loudly again. If the girl didn't watch out, she was going to hyperventilate right then and there. "That'd be great. I told my bridesmaids to wear their hats tonight, and now you can check and make sure they're on correctly. Oh, I feel so much better now."

With that, my young bride practically danced away from the gazebo, her ballet flats skimming the parched grass like a skater gliding over ice.

I leaned back on the bench. Now that I'd calmed my client, my work was done for the moment. I rested for another second, and then I rose as well, and began to walk back to the family chapel, where the wedding service would take place tomorrow night.

Like many of the antebellum homes here on the Great River Road, Honeycutt Hall contained a private family chapel for baptisms, weddings, and such. The chapel could hold about two dozen parishioners, which meant only close kin would be invited to the service. The party afterward, though, was another story. From what I'd heard of the plans, the bride had booked country band Rascal Flats—all three Flats, too, not just one of them—to entertain guests, followed by a local zydeco band, which guaranteed an all-night reverie.

The party matched the bride's spunky personality. While some might peg her as just another spoiled debutante, I enjoyed my client's quirky outlook. She was bright and inquisitive. The same, unfortunately, couldn't be said of her groom. The one and only time I'd met Wesley Carmichael—earlier today, at the final veil fitting—I found him cold and aloof. Not to mention a tad condescending.

But as Bo would say, there was no accounting for taste. Which he found to be true every time a client tried to foist an outrageous dress design on him. Like the time a Floridian wanted Bo to dress her as a mermaid, complete with a five-foot fin made of rainbow-colored rubber. Somehow, he accomplished it, although the girl had to be ferried down the aisle to her waiting groom.

No bother. Whether or not Wesley Carmichael enjoyed his wedding tomorrow night, I would. It wasn't every day I got to attend a client's ceremony, since I normally worked behind the scenes. And I had a very personal reason for wanting to attend the ceremony this time.

When Bo proposed to me last August, I thought I had oodles of time until the "big day" to plan my own nuptials. But then the calendar went into overdrive, and the days flew by faster and faster. As of today, I had only four weeks to finalize my wedding plans, which were sketchy, at best.

We managed to book one of the most beautiful venues in the area (hallelujah!) because I made a veil last year for the daughter of a steamship owner. The *Riverboat Queen* was a restored paddle-wheeler from the eighteen hundreds that looked like it belonged in a Mark Twain story, three levels high, with glossy red paint and a plethora of American flags. I fell in love with the ship the very first time I boarded her.

But we still had to choose the cake, plan the menu, and do all the thousand and one chores that went into creating a memorable ceremony. While I didn't have Lorelei's checkbook, I did have a strong work ethic, and I wasn't above "borrowing" some ideas from her reception. As everyone said, imitation was the sincerest form of flattery, and I planned to flatter the heck out of brides like Lorelei to plan my nuptials.

By the time I crossed the grounds of Honeycutt Hall, several other people had arrived at the property. One older couple looked like someone's grandparents, while I pegged a woman in sky-high stilettos standing next to them as a maiden aunt. I was just about to head for the family chapel when something touched my sleeve. Splashed against it, really. A tiny raindrop wobbled on my wrist, as if it couldn't decide whether to seep into the fabric or not. Bless Lorelei's heart! And this time, I meant it in the kindest way possible. No matter what anyone tried to tell you, rain was *not* a welcomed guest at a wedding. Especially one that included an outdoor reception, a tour bus full of electronic equipment, and a fireworks show set to blaze at midnight. Good luck? Hah! The only reason people ever told a bride about rainstorms and good luck was to make the girl stop crying. That was my opinion, anyway.

Sure enough, after a few more steps, another droplet joined the first. It was the start of a good old-fashioned thunderstorm, which often blew through southern Louisiana in the middle of July. Not only that, but the skies took on the yellowish tone of the mansion's walls, instead of the chalky white of the staircase, as God intended, which meant we were in for a real downpour.

"You're not listening to me!"

A man's voice thundered from behind a beautyberry hedge nearby. Apparently, I wasn't the only one discombobulated by the thunderstorm. I paused for a moment, until the gentleman spoke again.

"You never listen to me."

"I am *so* listening to you."

I recognized Lorelei's voice, with its deep-throated Cajun accent. Which meant she, no doubt, stood on the other side of the hedge with her fiancé.

I stretched on my tippy-toes to check out my hunch. Unfortunately, my vantage point was blocked by clumps of purple berries, so I sank to my heels again.

"Really, Lorelei?" her fiancé whined. "You've been listening to me? Okay, what did I just say?"

"Well, you..." Lorelei's voice trailed off miserably.

"See? I knew it." Her fiancé spat the words. "Not that you care, but my fever's up to a hundred degrees now."

"Ouch. Are you sure?"

"Of course I'm sure. I took it five minutes ago. And between the cough and my asthma, I can hardly breathe."

"Then I don't know what to do. Nana and Pop-Pop just got here, and they want to see you."

"We'll have to tell them no. I think I need to take a nap before the rehearsal."

"Maybe that's a good idea." Lorelei sounded pleased to have found something—anything—to hang her hat on. "I'm sure a long nap will do you wonders. You'd better take some Tylenol, too. I'll think of something to tell the guests. I'm sure they'll understand."

"Yes, but do you understand? I don't want to disappoint you since you've been working so hard on this wedding."

Well, butter my biscuit. Maybe Wesley Carmichael had a heart, after all. He sounded downright worried about his fiancée's feelings now. Maybe I'd judged him a bit too harshly.

"I understand," Lorelei said. "It's not your fault you got sick. And you've been so good to me when it comes to the wedding. C'mon…you even said yes to the roast beef, and you don't eat meat."

I was about to delicately cough, or clear my throat, or otherwise make my presence known—since lurking behind a beautyberry bush was *not* my idea of good client relations—when the heavens opened up for real. Rain splashed to the ground in sheets of palest silver; the individual droplets like daggers thrust from the clouds above.

"Eek!" Lorelei yelped.

While the couple raced to find shelter, I did the same. Already some strands of my hair fell into my eyes, and the rest wouldn't be far behind. So I hurried over to a staircase on the left, which led to a basement of some sort. A heavy oak door at the bottom of the staircase was cracked open a smidge, and, since the heavens showed no signs of a cease-fire, I ditched down the stairs and stumbled into the basement room.

Only to find out it wasn't a basement at all. The room housed an old wine cellar, which smelled of dried plant stalks and musky berries. Sure enough, a line of oak casks stairstepped up the wall, their centers cinched with iron staves. Someone had branded the sides with an elaborate "HH."

Everything else hid in the shadows, which didn't seem very safe to me, so I felt along the wall for the nearest light switch. Once I flicked the light on, the shadows immediately dissolved.

I was right…I stood in an ancient wine cellar, with an elaborately carved bar built into the far wall. Leave it to the Honeycutts to do everything top-notch, because the bar had the same HH monogram carved onto its side. Someone had even monogrammed the initials onto emerald-green seat cushions that topped a row of barstools.

As a final touch, a checkerboard of smooth mahogany shelves marched up the brick wall, designed to hold candlesticks, single-stem vases, or other interesting objects. A half-dozen shelves hopscotched up the wall in an elegant pattern. *Not a bad a place to ride out the storm.* The only thing that could make the room even cozier was the addition of my fiancé. But since that wasn't likely to happen, I settled onto one of the barstools and waited for the storm to pass. Little did I know how long the wait would be, or what would else would happen in that very room.

Chapter 2

The next morning dawned hot and bright, and the air sizzled with leftover moisture from last night's thundershowers.

I drove onto the grounds of Honeycutt Hall, accompanied by the cock-a-doodle-doo of a rooster. Since I rarely heard farm fowl back home in Bleu Bayou, it cheered my heart to be welcomed onto the property in such a unique way.

I continued down the pea-gravel lane—appropriately named Sugar Street, since the mansion's founders mined the crop in the eighteen hundreds—and entered a curved driveway that fronted the house. Once I found a parking spot, I stepped from my VW. I'd nicknamed the car Ringo in honor of another, more famous Beatle, and faint watermarks splashed my little bug from bumper to hood.

Thankfully, that seemed to be the only casualty from last night's thunderstorms, along with a few rain puddles on the gravel. Once the thundershowers finally disappeared last night, the wedding party went on to have a flawless rehearsal, capped by a champagne toast at midnight. Too bad the groom had to miss the festivities.

Other than that, everything was on track, as far as I could tell. I climbed the grand staircase to the first floor, and then I paused a moment to catch my breath.

Since Lorelei had invited me to spend the entire day at her house when we spoke at the rehearsal, I'd brought an arsenal of supplies with me: a carpenter's toolbox filled with beauty products, in case any of the bridesmaids needed a last-minute touch-up; a shoebox full of sewing supplies, including no-stick tape, several different spools of thread, and a chain of safety pins as long as my arm; an industrial-strength steamer for the lace veil; and my own gown for the occasion, which Bo chose for me. His pick? An Adrianna Papell sleeveless sheath with gold lace that stopped at the knees. A bit sassy and fun, it was formal enough to please even the most stalwart Southern hostess but cool enough to keep me comfortable during the reception, since July weddings in southern Louisiana could be notoriously steamy.

As a milliner, I couldn't attend such an important event bareheaded, though. In addition to the myriad boxes and bags I carried, I toted a hatbox with one of my favorite summer creations inside: a Parabuntal straw picture hat with a gold grosgrain bow. The simple design would complement the more ornate dress, while the wide brim would shield my face from the late-afternoon sun.

Thank goodness I spied someone standing on the other side of a window in the front door, and she opened the panel for me.

"Everyone's in the sunroom." She looked like the mother of the bride, with fair skin and chestnut hair. While I wore my auburn hair in an updo ninety percent of the time, this woman wore hers chin-length.

I happily relinquished my packages to her when she motioned for them. "Thank you so much. I'm the milliner, and I need to do some last-minute touch-ups on the bride's veil this morning. You must be Mrs. Honeycutt."

"Yes, indeed. Nice to meet you."

"I'm Melissa DuBois, but everyone calls me Missy. By the way, you have a lovely daughter."

"Thank you." Her smile broadened even more. "I'm quite partial to her myself. Now, everyone is already enjoying brunch in the sunroom, so please join them for a bite to eat."

At that moment, someone new entered the hall with her own armload of packages, so I cleared the way for my hostess to greet her next guest.

Once I said goodbye, I made my way down the hall, which featured oversized lanterns overhead, a white wainscoting that reached my waist on the walls, and honey-colored hardwoods underfoot. I followed the hardwoods into another room, this one built with floor-to-ceiling windows, used-brick floors, and enough greenery to fill an arboretum. I'd apparently reached the sunroom.

A half-dozen tables decorated the space, each topped with a linen cloth and magnolia centerpiece. One of the largest tables groaned under the weight of fruits, pastries, and enough orange juice to satisfy even a daycare center. I moved closer to the table, marveling at the size of the fruit, given that it was July and way past the end of the growing season.

Conversation buzzed around me. Most of the tables were full, and ones that weren't had purses or cell phones strewn across them as placeholders. I picked my way to a table on the right, where I recognized several of the bridesmaids and a groomsman or two.

"Do you mind if I sit here?" I addressed the nearest bridesmaid, who looked to be about Lorelei's age.

"Of course not." She edged her plate closer to her elbow. "You're the milliner, right? We were just talking about Lorelei's veil. It's gorgeous!"

"Thank you." I placed my lime-green clutch on the table and nodded at the buffet. "Now, if you don't mind, I'm going to grab one of those delicious-looking pastries. Would you like one, too?"

"No, I'm fine. I've been here for a while. I thought I'd see how Wesley's doing, but he hasn't come down yet. No one's seen him."

Uh-oh. That didn't sound good. From what I heard yesterday, his voice sounded like he'd been gargling with pea gravel, and the nasally tone signaled a head cold. He also mentioned a high fever to Lorelei.

"Oh, dear. I hope he's feeling better tonight."

The girl nodded noncommittally and returned to her breakfast, so I felt free to take my leave. I headed for the buffet table, where a stack of warmed plates anchored one end. Just as I was about to pull a plate off the top of the stack, I heard a loud clacking noise behind me. It sounded like a Clydesdale had entered the sunroom and clomped its way to the tables.

Sweet mother of pearl! The moment I turned, I thanked my lucky stars I wasn't wearing stilettos, because I would've toppled onto the buffet table. As it was, my mouth fell open and cool air rushed to the back of my throat.

There, next to a chocolate fountain surrounded by plump strawberries, stood Stormie Lanai, a local newscaster. She wore a pure-white pantsuit and leopard Manolo Blahniks that, no doubt, created the sound of horses' hooves.

Unfortunately, Stormie and I shared a long and complicated history, and I couldn't believe we both occupied the same space now.

It all began last fall. Stormie, a reporter for KATC in Baton Rouge, decided to return a veil I'd created for her wedding, exactly one week before her big day. She somehow landed a rich Texas oilman, and she planned to marry him at a renovated plantation as soon as possible. Those plans changed, however, when someone went missing there and police cordoned off the property. The resulting investigation forced her to come up with Plan B, which meant a Las Vegas wedding and a tiny fascinator instead of a floor-length veil. She couldn't understand why I wouldn't gladly refund her money, even though I'd spent months creating a beautiful cathedral-length train with carrickmacross lace and hundreds of tiny seed pearls. We finally resolved the matter with me taking apart the intricate veil and using the pieces to create a one-of-a-kind fascinator.

Stormie stood with her back to me now, as she picked among the strawberries by the fountain. I marshalled my courage, since there was no way we could avoid each other in a room this size, and I tapped her on the shoulder.

She instantly whirled around. "Why, Missy DuBois. Whatever are you doing here?"

Like always, Stormie wore so much foundation, her face resembled a Kabuki mask. As a newscaster, she was conditioned to wear heavy makeup for the cameras, but she'd never mastered the art of applying it in real life. Case in point, she wore false eyelashes so thick they resembled two butterflies about to take flight whenever she blinked, which was often.

"The bride hired me to make a wedding veil. What about you?"

"Why, I'm covering the wedding for Channel Eleven, of course. This shindig will be the biggest show our little state has ever seen!"

Leave it to Stormie to sound like a carnival barker as she described the Honeycutt wedding. No wonder she garnered such high ratings for KATC, since she tended to sensationalize everything she came across.

"Well, it was nice to see you again." I turned to leave, since even one minute with Stormie felt like ten times that amount.

"Just a second." She grabbed my arm before I could escape. "Have you heard my big news? I'm going to have a baby!"

"A baby?" I quickly glanced at her waist. Her flat-panel pants hugged her hips tightly and showed only a bit of a telltale bump. "That's wonderful! How far along are you?"

"Just a few weeks. But I couldn't wait to share my big news. And it's going to be a Christmas baby. We're thinking of naming her Holly, if it's a girl, or Nicholas, if it's a boy."

"Those are great names." Whether or not Stormie and I saw eye to eye on most things, my heart always melted whenever the conversation turned to babies. "I'm sure y'all will find just the right name. I'm very happy for you and your husband. Now, if you don't mind, I really should be going."

With that, I delicately extricated my arm and made my way back to the right side of the room. By now, several of the bridesmaids had left my table, with only a few leftover crumbs to testify to their presence.

Speaking of which, I had completely forgotten to grab a pastry! Seeing Stormie again had rattled me so, I could barely remember my own name, let alone to grab a beignet or two.

With a sigh, I turned again. Luckily, Stormie had disappeared, and someone new stood in her stead. It was Mrs. Honeycutt, only now she looked terribly upset.

I gingerly approached her. "Are you okay?" I couldn't imagine things could have changed that much since we met in the hall.

"No. No, I'm not." She looked at me with drowning eyes. "Something's terribly wrong."

"Wrong?" Earlier, she seemed so calm and collected, as if she hosted fancy get-togethers every day. But now, she seemed frazzled, as if she didn't know what to do first. "What's happened?"

"No one can find Wesley. He isn't in his room, and no one's seen him this morning. I sent our houseman to go look for him, but he hasn't found him yet."

Something about the mother's distress pulled at my heartstrings. Of all the things for the mother-of-the-bride to face on the day of her daughter's wedding, a missing fiancé should *not* be one of them.

"Please let me help you. I'm not busy right now, and you must have a million other things to worry about."

"Oh, dear. That would be wonderful." Her relief quickly gave way to doubt, though. "But I couldn't possibly ask you to do that. You should be our guest today."

"Nonsense. I'm happy to help you. Where did you say the houseman went?"

"I didn't, but he's over there." She quickly pointed to the nearest window.

An elderly man stood on the other side of it, wearing navy coveralls and a tool belt slung low on his waist. Something about the getup sparked a hazy memory, but it refused to crystallize.

"Great. I'll go talk to him." I hurried away from the sunroom and followed the hall to the front door. Once I moved outside and traipsed down the stairs, I spotted the houseman in a side garden. Even with his back to me, something about his posture looked oddly familiar.

"Hello, there," I called.

The moment he turned, the memory solidified. It was Darryl Tibodeaux, the Cajun caretaker from Morningside Plantation. Darryl and I met three years ago, when a bride disappeared the night before her wedding at the plantation. Darryl worked as a groundskeeper, and he and I bonded during the police investigation.

Time hadn't changed a thing. Darryl's coveralls still wore a fine layer of potting soil, and his thinning hair exposed a pale, freckled scalp. He recognized me right away, too. "Miz DuBois!"

He hurried over and thrust out his left hand, since the sleeve on his right side was empty. Darryl lost the appendage in a horrible accident at an oil refinery, but he refused to be bitter about it. In fact, he could hoist things that were so heavy they would challenge a man half his age.

"No need to be so formal, Darryl." I smiled and gave him a quick hug. "Last I heard, you were managing an arboretum in Alabama." In addition to being a top-notch handyman, Darryl possessed a love of plants that inspired me to start my own garden back home. "What made you decide to come back?"

He winked. "Dat's water under da bridge. I missed ma people too much ta stay away."

"So, now you're working here?" I was stating the obvious, since an embroidered HH decorated his coveralls, but I didn't care. I was just so happy to see him.

"Yes, ma'am. Come back las' month. Got da job here wit' da Honeycutts now."

"Darryl, that's so wonderful! I guess you can take the man out of Louisiana—"

"But not da Louisiana outta da man," he finished for me.

The minute our conversation lagged, I remembered why I came outside in the first place.

"Say, Darryl, I'm afraid Mrs. Honeycutt sent me out here to help you. She's worried sick about her daughter's fiancé, and she thought I might be able to help you find him."

His aqua eyes slanted a bit. "It don' look good, ta tell you da truth. I covered da house from top ta bottom, and most a' da fields out back."

"Hmmm." It seemed to me Darryl would have a handle on the best places for someone to hide if he wanted some peace and quiet. Especially someone who wasn't feeling well. "So, what's left to search?"

"I was abou' ta look at da silos." He nodded at the twin water towers that bookended the mansion. Two stories tall, they resembled thin, pastel pagodas that stood watch over the property.

"But how will you get inside?" I peered at the nearest one, which faced east.

"Look closer. Deys got doors on der backs."

Sure enough, someone had carved three-foot-high doors into the backsides of the towers, and crude wood handles kept the panels in place.

"I see. Why don't we divide and conquer? I'll check the one on the right, and you can check the one on the left."

He nodded, apparently satisfied with the plan. "Meet ya back here. And be careful, Miz Dubois. No tellin' what's inside dem."

I gulped, since I hadn't even thought about what could be lurking in the structures. For all I knew, the towers could be home to a family of possums, a fez of armadillo, or worse. At least the structures were close to the house, so everyone would hear if I let out a bloodcurdling scream.

We turned, and, like two gunfighters in a duel, we each took a dozen paces to our respective water tower. Being July, the ground had hardened, even with last night's showers, and my flats slapped against the hardpacked earth. Once again, I thanked my lucky stars I wasn't wearing stilettos, because my toe caught on the exposed root of a pin oak on my way to the tower, and it nearly upended me.

After I regained my balance, I appraised the silo in front of me. In addition to a simple door that covered the opening, a turret spiraled from the roof of the tower, and it was made of horizontal slats that allowed water to seep into a holding tank. It was quite charming, actually, given the sunny yellow paint on the walls and peacock-blue turret on top.

I paused in front of the door. One twist of the handle and it slowly swung open, emitting a loud and high-pitched squeak.

My, but it's dark inside. I automatically reached for the flashlight app on my cell phone. Once I trained it into the darkness, it pierced the black with a shaft of light. I leaned as far as I could into the opening, since I had no desire to wiggle into the tank and come across a curious marsupial or two.

I waved the phone at the walls, but they all looked perfectly normal to me. A sheet of aluminum covered them, and mineral deposits freckled the surface. The storms last night had added about a half-inch of water to the tank, and a lone ladder stretched from the concrete floor to the roof. Apparently, no one had used it in quite some time, because cobwebs crisscrossed the ladder's rungs.

Just when I was about to shut off my phone and cry "uncle," I noticed something navy lying against the far side of the ladder. It looked like one of Darryl's coveralls, which he must've tossed into the tower at some point and forgotten about.

"Interesting," I said, more to myself than anyone else.

"What's dat?"

The voice startled me so much, I dropped my cell phone and it lurched toward the water.

"Oh, sugar!" I quickly dove for it. Luckily, my reflexes saved the phone from a watery death, and I scooped it up in the nick of time.

"Ya shouldn't drop yer phone like dat." It was Darryl again, who hadn't moved from his spot behind me.

"And you shouldn't scare the bejesus out of me." I took a deep breath to calm my nerves. "Okay, then. Did you find anything in your water tower?"

"Nuthin' but sum fresh rain and spiders. You?"

"Same. Oh, and you might want to check your supply of coveralls. I think you left one over there." I pointed my cell into the maw, which illuminated the pile of clothing I'd spotted earlier.

"I don' keep nuthin' in here. I gots a supply closet for dat."

Now it was my turn to look confused. "So, what's that over there?"

We both reached the same conclusion at the same time.

"Aaaiiieee!" we screamed, the noise ping-ponging around the tower like machine-gun fire.

The moment we finished, our individual instincts kicked in. I moved aside so Darryl could hop into the tower ahead of me. Bravery was one thing, but foolhardiness was quite another, and Darryl knew the towers much better than I did. Once he disappeared into the darkness, I did the same. He bent to inspect the pile of clothes as the rainwater puddled around his ankles.

"Don't tell me—" I trained the phone lower to give Darryl a better view.

"Yep, it's da boy 'sposed to be gettin' married today."

My heart fell. Of all the horrible discoveries to make, this one took the cake. While I'd uncovered more than my fair share of bodies here on the Great River Road, not one of them was a groom. I could only imagine how Lorelei would feel on what should've been one of the happiest days of her life.

Darryl extended his shaking hand to Wesley's body and placed two fingers against the groom's neck. When he quickly withdrew his hand, I knew there was no hope.

"Dead?" I asked.

"Yep. Cold as ice."

"What should we do?" The moment I said it, though, I knew the answer. It was time to call Lance LaPorte, one of my oldest and dearest friends, who served as a detective with the Louisiana State Police Department. Lance would know what to do.

Once again, he'd innocently take my call and breezily ask about my morning, never once imagining I was about to report a dead body. It had happened time and time again. And every time I thought I had found the last one, I'd stumble across another victim.

I wouldn't blame Lance if he blocked my calls permanently and "unfriended" me from his life.

Chapter 3

Contrary to my opinion, Lance answered my phone call right away, and he sounded pleased as punch to hear from me. "Hey, there. How're you doing?"

"I've been better, to be honest. Lots better."

"Uh-oh. I don't like that tone. What's up?"

"I'll tell you, but you have to promise a few things." I quickly composed a mental list of all the worst-case scenarios. "Number one: you can't hang up. I don't think I could take that this morning. Number two: you can't think I'm cursed or anything."

"I really don't like where this is heading." His voice sounded wary, although I couldn't blame him.

"Okay, here goes." I took a deep breath and plunged ahead. "I may have found another dead body."

"What do you mean...may? Either you did, or you didn't. Which is it?"

"The first. I'm here at Honeycutt Hall. Hey...you'll never guess who works here now. It's—"

"Uh, Missy? First things first. Tell me about your discovery." Like always, Lance switched into cop mode the instant I mentioned a dead body.

"It's the groom for a wedding here today. His name is Wesley Carmichael."

"Any trauma you can see?"

"I didn't really look." While I didn't want to sound abrupt, my tone was totally understandable. I had no intention of getting any closer to a corpse than absolutely necessary.

"Is anyone else with you?" Lance had obviously switched tacks.

"As a matter of fact, there is. It's that employee I started to tell you about. Only you wouldn't let me finish. Now would you?"

Luckily, Lance and I treated each other like family, and neither of us took offense when the other one became snippy. Although now wasn't the time, nor the place, for family bickering.

"So, who's there with you?" he repeated.

"It's Darryl. Darryl Tibodeaux. Remember him? He was the groundskeeper at Morningside Plantation." I glanced at Darryl, who stood stock still next to me.

Apparently, Darryl had no intention of moving closer to the corpse, either.

"Of course I remember him," Lance said. "Could you please put him on the phone?"

I silently handed Darryl the cell. "It's Lance LaPorte on the phone," I whispered. "He's that detective with the Louisiana State Police Department."

Darryl nodded and took the cell in his left hand. He seemed resigned to answering the questions I couldn't field.

"Hello?" Darryl waited a moment, and then he glanced over his shoulder at the body. "No signs a' trauma. Looks like he's been sleepin.' Like he come in here ta take da nap."

Another moment passed as Lance asked him more questions.

"Yes, sir," Darryl answered. "I felt his neck. Da skin is cold and stiff. Like it's frozen or sumptin'."

Apparently, that description told Lance everything he needed to know, because Darryl silently passed the phone back to me.

"Well?" I asked Lance. "Are you coming out here or not? By the way, we're in one of the water towers by the main house. The one on the right if you're facing the front door."

"I'll be there in about twenty minutes," Lance said. "Stay put, okay?"

Although the idea didn't thrill me, I knew it was for the best. Better to stay near a body than tramp around the scene and mess up the evidence. There'd be time enough to tell Lorelei and her mother about our discovery once Lance arrived at the house.

"Please hurry up. There's supposed to be this big wedding here today and everyone's already worried because they can't find the groom."

"I'm on my way." With that, Lance clicked off the line, leaving me to answer Darryl's questioning looks as best I could.

"Looks like we need to stay here until Lance arrives. But, for goodness' sake, at least let's move outside the tower. This place is giving me the heebie-jeebies."

With that, Darryl and I carefully picked our way back through the doorway and stepped into daylight. It looked like it was going to be a very long day, and neither of us looked forward to it.

* * * *

Twenty minutes later, Lance's Buick Oldsmobile pulled up to the mansion, the removable lightbar on its roof twirling silently in the morning light. As always, the car wore a coat of red mud on the undercarriage that extended from one wheel well to the other. One of these days I'd convince Lance to visit the Sparkle N' Shine car wash in town, but not today.

By the time he arrived, I'd already called Ambrose at his design studio and filled him in on the morning's events. My fiancé offered to drop everything and race out to Honeycutt Hall to be with me, but I talked him out of it. There was nothing he could do. Plus, he needed time at his studio to catch up on all his wedding orders, since we were smack-dab in the middle of the wedding season and Saturday was the busiest day of the week.

Once I calmed Ambrose, I hung up the phone and rehearsed what I could possibly say to Lance. By now, the detective knew me as the girl with the uncanny ability to find dead bodies. It was a reputation I didn't ask for, and I surely didn't want.

He appeared on the scene in his casual clothes, which included a pair of khakis and a navy polo. He strode across the browned grass, to where Darryl and I stood.

"Lance." I nodded stiffly, since I knew my role by now.

While Lance and I normally joked about everything and anything, that changed the minute a police investigation commenced. Now, I was a witness and he was my interrogator, and I learned a long time ago not to take his strict tone personally.

"Missy." He returned the nod. "And Darryl. I haven't seen you in a long time. How've you been?"

"Good," Darryl said. "Until today, dat is."

"I understand. Why don't you come with me, and I'll ask you a few questions."

Lance led Darryl over to a patch of grass just out of earshot. I knew he'd separate us when he arrived, since that was the first thing a detective did when he or she came across multiple witnesses. That way, my recollection wouldn't interfere with Darryl's memories, and his memories wouldn't color my statement.

The two men returned a few minutes later.

"Your turn." Lance led me to the same spot where he had questioned Darryl.

"This is something, isn't it?" I said. "I never dreamed I'd find another dead body when I came out here today."

He nodded. "You have quite the talent for it. Why *did* you come out here today?"

"Lorelei Honeycutt is one of my clients. I made her veil for the ceremony today. She invited me to come out early, and I took her up on it. I wanted to tweak the bridesmaids' hats and steam Lorelei's veil before the ceremony. Guess that's not going to happen now."

Lance watched my face as he scribbled something onto a small notepad. He told me something a long time ago I'd never forgotten: a detective will study the face of a witness to determine whether she's lying or not. If the person glances right, it means she's pulling something from her memory. But if she glances left, it means she's lying. Although I didn't think Lance would question my truthfulness, he must've gotten so used to watching a witness that he did it as a matter of course now.

"I feel just awful about this," I said. "Lorelei Honeycutt is such a sweet girl, and her mother is precious."

"Hmmm. I've never dealt with them before."

That didn't surprise me. Like me, Lance originally hailed from Texas, and he'd only been working as a police detective for three years or so.

"What do you think happened to the groom?" I asked.

"I'll know more once I examine the body. To the best of your knowledge, did anyone come or go from the water tower this morning?"

"Not that I know of. The door was shut tight, and nothing looked out of place. At first, I thought Wesley's body was only a puddle of clothes. One of Darryl's coveralls, to be exact. I have no idea how he ended up there, Lance."

Lance flipped the notepad closed. Once he shoved it back in his pocket, he started to return to Darryl.

The houseman was still waiting for us by the tower, and he seemed relieved when Lance told him he could leave the scene.

"But please don't mention this to anyone yet," Lance said. "I want to be the one to break the news to the family."

That was another tidbit I'd learned from Lance about police investigations. A detective assigned to a case normally told the family about someone's death, so he or she could study the reactions of the next of kin. Some people were incredible actors, and they faked grief at the drop of a hat, while other people were unable to hide their emotions. Lance once apprehended a woman who murdered her husband, and she implicated herself when she couldn't stop giggling during the interview. While that was an extreme case, it encouraged Lance to take the lead and announce a death himself. Once Darryl walked away, I turned to him. "You know, this is going to devastate the bride. Even though..."

Lance watched me carefully. "Even though what?"

"Well, it's probably nothing." I was unable to shake the memory of Lorelei and Wesley arguing behind the hedge. "But I overhead the bride and groom fighting yesterday." Far be it from me to keep any information I had from Lance. He trusted me to be as forthright as possible, and it was one of the reasons he'd include me in these investigations.

"What were they fighting about?"

"Apparently, Wesley felt sick, and he didn't think he could make it to the rehearsal last night."

"Did he?"

"No, he didn't. Lorelei's dad had to stand in for him. I thought he would stay in bed this morning to recuperate. I think that's what a lot of people expected."

"Interesting." Lance whipped out his notepad again and wrote something else down. "I think it's time we headed for the house."

I didn't look back as we walked across the grass. I knew the next time I saw the area, yellow caution tape would separate it from the rest of the property. To be honest, I wanted to forget the view of Wesley lying face-down in a half-inch of water, his body twisted around the base of the ladder like a wadded-up blanket.

So I remained silent as we made our way to the house. Halfway there, something else caught my attention. The stairwell that led to the wine cellar—the same stairwell I took yesterday to avoid the rain—was now blocked by a small statue. A winged statue of an angel about to take flight. Like the rest of the property, the statue looked expensive but timeworn.

"Well, that's weird." I paused by the stairwell, my thoughts retreating to last night's thunderstorm. I definitely didn't run across a blockade when I ducked down the stairs and ran into the wine cellar. Someone purposefully blocked the path now. But, why?

"What's weird?" Lance asked.

"That statue wasn't here last night. The staircase leads to a wine cellar, and I went downstairs when it started to pour."

"That *is* strange." Lance didn't hesitate. He automatically bent to move the statue out of the way. Although it didn't look heavy, his shoulders strained with the effort.

"Here, let me help you." I placed both hands on the wings and gave a hearty push.

Once the statue ended up on the grass, Lance hopped ahead of me and went down the steps. I followed him, and my eyesight automatically dimmed as I entered the shadowy cellar.

There, across the room, hulked the long bar I'd spied earlier, with the initials HH carved into the wood. Across from it was the display of casks that stairstepped up the wall. Everything looked the same. Everything, that was, except for two of the barstools, which had been moved to a side table by the wall. The monogrammed stools sat cheek by jowl in a shadowy corner of the room.

"I'll hit the lights." I reached for the switch I found yesterday and fired up the chandeliers behind the bar. Sure enough, the barstools had been moved to a high-top table that sat by the casks.

"That's different." I made my way over there. The table was dented and nicked, an obvious antique, and the legs didn't quite match up, so it leaned forward a bit.

"What's different about it?" Lance joined me by the table and placed his hands on his hips. He'd already given the room a brief once-over. Knowing him, nothing escaped his notice, and he'd probably observed several things I hadn't even seen.

"It's just that someone moved the chairs." I pointed to the monogrammed seats. "And it had to happen after I left the room. I think it was about nine by the time the rain stopped and I finally went inside the house."

"Wasn't there a wedding rehearsal last night?' Lance asked. "I always thought they hold those earlier in the evening, because the minister has to come out, too."

"Usually, yes. But this one didn't start until later. And it didn't get over until midnight. I remember that because the bride's father gave a toast, and he talked about the late hour."

"Maybe some of the wedding party came back here after the rehearsal." Lance seemed to be talking more to himself than me, because he spoke softly as he appraised the chairs.

"Could be, but most people were talking about going straight to bed after the toast. We were all pretty tired by that point."

Lance bent to inspect the table more closely. Just when I thought he was about to touch it, his gaze darted sideways, to a ledge built into the stone wall. I glanced at it as well, and spied two wineglasses tucked on the wood outcropping. Something watery and red colored the bowls of the wineglasses, and ruby liquid dribbled down the sides.

We both moved closer to a get a better look. Sure enough, the remnants of a merlot, cabernet, or some other crimson wine stained the glasses. "What do you make of that?" I didn't recall seeing the glasses the night before. I remembered seeing the shelves, which staggered up the stone walls, but I didn't remember them holding anything.

"I'd say someone had a little party here." Lance didn't touch the glasses. Instead, he removed his cell from his pocket and snapped several pictures. "I need to get my investigator in here to take some measurements before I move these. You said you didn't notice them last night?"

"No, I didn't. I remember liking the shelves because they added character, but I don't remember seeing anything on them."

"Okay, then." Once he reappraised the barstools and table, Lance suddenly squatted.

"What's wrong?"

He must've spotted something on the ground.

With a quick motion, Lance withdrew some latex gloves from the pocket of his khakis. Once he put them on, he picked up something small, white, and rectangular from the floor. It looked like a piece of paper, or perhaps a wrapper of some sort.

He studied it, too, before he placed it in a plastic evidence bag he kept in the same pocket as the gloves. When he finally zippered the bag shut, he turned to me. "It's a paper someone would use to roll a cigarette. But someone must've dropped it under the barstool."

"I don't smell smoke. Wouldn't you think we'd have noticed that?"

"Maybe it wasn't tobacco." Lance shoved the evidence bag into the pocket of his khakis and turned to leave. "No one said it had to be a regular cigarette. Plus, we don't know what time someone dropped the paper. Maybe the smell had a chance to dissolve."

"Hmmm."

Once again, Lance had managed to think of things I hadn't even considered.

He continued to walk. "C'mon, Missy," he said over his shoulder. "I think it's time to go tell the family what's happened. I'm going to come back here afterward and seal up the room. You're free to go if you want, though. I know it's been a trying morning."

"Oh, no. I'm going with you." To be honest, I didn't relish the thought of going home to an empty house, since Ambrose planned to work at his studio all day. If anything, I wanted to help the family at Honeycutt Hall. In a few minutes, Lorelei would hear the worst news of her life, and I wanted to be there to help her family pick up the pieces.

Chapter 4

Once Lance closed up the wine cellar and returned the statue to its place at the head of the stairs, we headed over to the house.

Just as we were about to ascend the grand staircase, my cell phone buzzed in my pocket, and I quickly withdrew it.

"Hello?" The number on the screen looked vaguely familiar, although I couldn't quite place it.

"Uh, is this Missy DuBois?" The caller swallowed her words, the way Lorelei and the other Cajuns around here did.

I didn't recognize the voice, though. "It is. I'm afraid this isn't a good time—"

"I'm sorry to bother you, but this is important." The girl's words were sharp. Whatever she had to say obviously couldn't wait. "I'm Brandy d'Aulnay."

A-ha. The d'Aulnays owned the paddle-wheeler where Ambrose and I planned to be married in a few weeks. "Are you one of Mr. d'Aulnay's daughters?" The man had five of them, so odds were good she belonged to the family.

"I am. I'm the middle child, and I work for my dad, too."

I'd only run across three d'Aulnays during my time on the Great River Road. The first was Mr. d'Aulnay, who was a successful businessman and someone who liked to throw his weight around. The second was Sabine d'Aulnay, who hired me to make a veil for her wedding last year.

For some reason, Sabine elected to get married in a church, instead of on her father's riverboat, although I had no idea why. Finally, I also worked with the matriarch of the family when I booked the reservation for my wedding.

"I know you worked with my mom a few months ago," Brandy said. "But I'm afraid I have terrible news."

"News?" I couldn't imagine what that might be. Had they double-booked the venue? Decided to raise their rates? My mind swirled with possibilities.

"There's no easy way to say this. A fire broke out on the *Riverboat Queen* last night, and it gutted the ship's kitchen. I'm afraid we have to cancel all special events for the next few months."

Fire? "But…but…that's not possible. I put down a deposit and everything."

"I know you did, and I'm so sorry about this. It's the same story for everyone. All of our bookings have to go somewhere else until we can repair the ship."

"But that can't be right." Something inside me refused to accept the news. The words didn't make sense. They tumbled end over end, weightless and out of order. "There must be some mistake. Surely it won't take you several months to repair a little fire damage. How bad can it be?"

"It destroyed the whole electrical system. My dad redid it not too long ago, but it must've short-circuited during the night. We're not quite sure how the fire started. We called our insurance agent, and he's coming out today."

"I see." My mind still reeled from the news. "Can't we just move everything to the top deck?"

"No, I'm afraid that's not possible. Without the kitchen, you can't have the reception onboard. Even if you brought in food, you'd need water hookups and electricity, and they're both turned off. Again, I'm so sorry this happened, but you'll have to find another venue."

"I understand." Finally, I relented. It was painfully obvious no amount of talking on my part was going to fix the situation, no matter how much I wished it would. "Well, thank you for letting me know."

"You could always push back your wedding date." She sounded hopeful, as if she was helping the situation.

"I don't think so." After knowing Ambrose for more than three years, and enduring more than our fair share of ups and downs, I couldn't imagine delaying the ceremony any longer. Already it felt as if we'd waited a lifetime to be married, and I didn't have the patience to hold out anymore.

"The Queen should be back in business by fall," Brandy said. "Winter, at the very latest. That's all I can tell you for now. Goodbye."

The minute she hung up the phone, I let the cell fall to my side. Of all the things for someone to tell me this morning, that was the last one I expected.

"What's up?" Lance could read my face like a book, and he knew right away something was wrong.

"That was one of the d'Aulnays. They're the family that owns the *Riverboat Queen.* My goodness, Lance...the ship burned last night. I can't have my wedding there next month."

Although we were in a rush, Lance stopped in his tracks and draped his arm around my shoulders. "That's too bad. But if I know you, Missy—and I do—you'll find another place."

"I don't know. It's really late in the season, and everything else is already booked up." Unlike him, I had my doubts. "Ambrose and I both loved that venue. We even paid half up front to hold the booking."

"I'm sure they'll refund your money."

Lance remained at my side, which I appreciated. Even though duty called, he put everything aside to comfort me in my time of need. That was why he was my best friend and always would be.

"But this changes everything." I tried not to pout, but the whine came out anyway. "I already mailed the invitations."

"That's okay. We can call people. Maybe if we got a group together, we could go through your guest list and let everyone know."

I paused long enough to consider that. To be honest, it didn't sound half bad. When I first moved to Bleu Bayou, I didn't know a soul. But I'd managed to make lots of friends since then, including my assistant, Beatrice; Lance's mother, who owned a wonderful restaurant in town; and a fun-loving cakemaker named Bettina. Most of my friends worked in the wedding industry, and they could work magic when it came to special events. Maybe I could call on them to help me spread the word and even brainstorm ideas for a new venue.

"Maybe," I said. "But first things first. I need to call Ambrose and let him know what's going on."

"Okay, then. Why don't you stay here and do that. I'll go to the house and talk to the family."

"Wait." Much as I wanted to speak to Ambrose and tell him about the recent turn of events, it wouldn't change anything. Whether I called him now, or an hour from now, we still couldn't use the paddle-wheeler for our wedding. "I think I'll go inside with you. I can always call Bo afterward."

"Are you sure?"

"Positive. Besides, he's probably busy with a client right now. No need to ruin his morning when he's at work."

"Okay, then. Let's go." Lance took my arm and began to lead me away from the wine cellar. "To be honest, I hate this part of my job. You never know how people are going to react when you tell them you've found a body."

We walked in silence to the grand staircase, and then we ascended it to the first floor. Once again, I spotted Lorelei's mother through a window at the entrance. She stood in the foyer, ready to welcome more guests to her home, but she froze the moment she saw me.

Slowly, she opened the door and leaned out. "Is something wrong, dear?"

Apparently, I'd make a terrible poker player, because my mood always showed up on my face. "Well, um..."

Lance saved me by stepping in between us.

"Hello." He quickly withdrew his police badge from his front pocket. "I'm Lance LaPorte with the Louisiana PD. Could I speak with Lorelei Honeycutt, please?"

Mrs. Honeycutt stared hard at the badge, as if she'd never seen one before, which she probably hadn't. When she glanced up again, her eyes looked even more troubled. "What's this about, Officer?"

"I'd like to give everyone the news at once. Please find Lorelei and the rest of the wedding party. Is there a room we could use? Something private?"

"Yes. Of course." She sounded reticent, although I couldn't blame her. It wasn't every day a police officer arrived on one's doorstep. "Please come inside, Officer. Hello again, Missy."

"Hello, Mrs. Honeycutt." My smile felt strained as I returned her greeting.

"Please call me Nelle. And you can use the room at the end of the hall." She pointed to the sunroom. "Missy, you know how to find it."

"Thank you," Lance said. "We'll be waiting there."

While Nelle left to gather the wedding party, I took Lance to the sunroom, with its massive windows and expansive view. By now, it looked completely different, though. Gone were the tables draped in linen and stocked with plates of biscuits, fruit, and whatnot. Instead, a set of white wicker furniture decorated the space, including a sofa, which wore a plaid cushion; several armchairs, with backs that fanned out from the seats; and a large glass coffee table. A worker had begun to dismantle the last of the buffet tables, and he stood amid a pile of serving utensils he'd placed on the ground.

"Excuse me." Lance approached him. "We're going to have a meeting here." He pulled out his badge and held it up for the man's benefit. "I need you to leave the room for an hour or so."

The worker looked surprised, but he nodded and gathered up the utensils. Then he quickly headed down the hall and disappeared around a corner.

He was immediately replaced by someone new.

A young man in his twenties came ambling along, his penny loafers squeaking against the hardwoods. "Hello, there. I heard we're going to have a little powwow in here." The stranger extended his hand. "Name's Buck Liddell. I get to be the best man at this little shindig."

I cautiously placed my hand in his. He sounded awfully sunny for such a serious meeting, although he didn't know why Lance was there.

"Nice to meet you. I'm Melissa DuBois, and this is Detective Lance LaPorte with the Louisiana Police Department."

His mood instantly changed. "Whoa. To what do we owe the pleasure, Officer?"

Lance held up the badge again. "There's been some news this morning."

Buck carefully studied Lance's ID. Unlike the rest of us, he was dressed to the nines this morning. He wore expensive linen trousers with knife-sharp pleats, a striped dress shirt cinched at the wrists with heirloom cuff links, and a Rolex diver's watch as big as one of the biscuits put out for breakfast.

"Please have a seat, Mr. Liddell," Lance said.

Since Buck was the first to arrive, he had his choice of chairs, and he selected the sofa placed front and center. He plopped onto the cushion and looked at Lance expectantly. "Can you give me a hint? I mean, c'mon. It has to be about the wedding, right? Why else would you be here?"

When Lance didn't respond, Buck leaned forward. "Don't tell me old Wesley finally got himself in trouble. I told him he was going to get in hot water if he stayed with that crowd."

"That crowd?" Lance calmly leveled his gaze at the man. By now, he'd heard everything there was to hear under the sun, so nothing caught him off guard.

"Yeah. The people down at the racetrack. They don't take it lightly when you can't cover a bet. Let me guess…he had to light out of town because his bookie was after him."

"Mr. Liddell." Lance spoke firmly this time. Apparently, he'd tired of Buck's guessing game. "It's even more serious than that. There's been a death on the property."

"Oh." The words slapped the smirk right off Buck's face. Instead of making a witty comeback, he flopped against the cushion, dumbfounded. "Holy s—"

Just then, someone new entered the room. It was a handsome Chinese man, who carried an empty vase and a roll of green florist's tape. "What's going on?" He approached Lance. "I was told to drop everything and get over here."

The stranger wore a faux-fur vest that seemed wildly out of place for a house in the country, not to mention for the steamy weather.

"That's right," Lance said. "Please have a seat. And you are…"

"Jamison Lee. I own a flower shop in town. You can call me Jamie."

I blinked at the name. I'd heard of him before...but where?

"Hello, there," I said. "I'm Melissa DuBois. I think we both worked on the same wedding a while ago. It's been months, but it took place in Las Vegas. I made the bride's hat, and I heard she flew you in to make the centerpieces."

"You must be talking about Stormie Lanai." He rolled his eyes at the memory. "Now *that* was an interesting wedding."

"You don't say." I smiled, despite the solemn occasion, because I knew exactly what he was talking about. "You're very diplomatic. I also found her to be—as you put it—interesting."

"I'm sure you did. You own Crowning Glory, right? Everyone's talking about the great work you do at your shop."

"Thank you." Although this didn't seem like the time, nor the place, for small talk, I couldn't exactly ignore his compliment. "I've heard wonderful things about you, too."

Lance cleared his throat, obviously ready to get down to business. "You can sit over there on the sofa, Mr. Lee."

The florist shrugged and sank onto the small sofa, next to Buck Liddell. The best man barely acknowledged him, although I could tell they knew each other by their body language. Buck turned sideways, as if he didn't want anything to do with the florist, while Jamie seemed amused by the snub.

Within a few minutes, the room had filled. Darryl walked in holding a pair of garden clippers, which he compulsively cleaned on the side of his coveralls. The bridesmaid from breakfast—the one who so graciously welcomed me to her table—inched into the space as if pulled along by a rope. The last to enter were Lorelei and Nelle, who linked arms as if they were facing a firing squad.

Jamie came to Lorelei's rescue by indicating a spot next to him on the small sofa. She immediately left her mother's side to join him on the sofa.

By now, everyone had found a place to sit, or they'd resigned themselves to standing against the wall. All in all, about twenty people milled around the sunroom, most of them looking extremely ill at ease.

"Thank you all for coming," Lance began.

I noticed he carefully appraised each member of the wedding party as he spoke.

"Please don't make us wait any longer, Officer." Nelle's voice was soft but firm. She'd moved behind the sofa, as if she could protect Lorelei that way.

"There's no easy way to say this." Lance weighed his words carefully. "I understand everyone's been looking for the groom this morning. That you were afraid Wesley Carmichael had gone AWOL."

"He wouldn't do that!" A gentleman in the back of the room leaned forward in his seat. "My son wouldn't leave his bride at the altar. That's not who he is."

A-ha. Wesley's father. Mr. Carmichael's face slowly reddened, and several people tried to gently coax him back into his seat. He shook off their efforts as if they were flies that buzzed around his shoulders.

"I have news about your son." Lance waited for Mr. Carmichael to regain his composure before he continued. "He didn't abandon his fiancée. We found his body this morning, right here on the property."

Someone gasped at the back of the room. The next sound I heard was a soft thud as a body fell to the ground. It seemed to come from the back of the room, near Mr. Carmichael.

I craned my neck to peer over several heads. Sure enough, the old man remained seated—but a woman bedside him had fallen to the floor. Wesley's mother, perhaps?

"Get that woman some air." Lance moved to the back of the room. "Don't crowd around her."

He rushed over to the fallen woman and gently rolled her onto her back. Then he carefully loosened a bow she'd tied at her neck and undid the first few buttons of her silk blouse.

"Let's sit her up." Lance nodded at one of the groomsmen, who hovered nearby, and together they eased Mrs. Carmichael into a sitting position. "We need to get her upstairs, to her room." Lance motioned to another man; this one also in the wedding party. "You, there. Grab her other arm."

"That's okay." Mr. Carmichael quickly stood and inserted himself between Lance and the groomsman. "She's my wife. It's my responsibility."

"No," Lance said firmly. "Let these other guys do it. No offense, but I want to make sure she gets there safely."

With that, the two strapping groomsmen lifted Mrs. Carmichael by the shoulders and hoisted her to her feet. By this time, she'd come around, and her head lolled back and forth as she was guided from the room.

Her husband tried to leave, as well.

"I'd like you to stay here, Mr. Carmichael," Lance said. "I need to speak with you, if you don't mind."

"But..." The older man looked confused, as if he didn't know which way to turn. After a few moments, he seemed to bow to Lance's wishes. "Of course, Officer. Whatever you say."

I quickly snuck a glance at the bride. She hadn't budged from her spot on the small sofa, although she looked ashen.

I worried that maybe she'd gone into shock, so I quickly stepped in front of the sofa. "Lorelei? Are you all right?"

She glanced at me, but her stare was vacant. I'd found that sometimes it helped to touch a person who'd just received bad news, since it seemed to ground them to the here and now and kept them from slipping away.

I softly placed my hand on her knee. "It's going to be okay. You're going to be all right."

She didn't respond, though. It was almost as if she couldn't hear me.

"Now see here, Officer LaPorte." It was the florist, who spoke so loudly, both Lorelei and I flinched. "Are you sure it was Wesley? How do you know you didn't make a mistake? It could've been someone else."

"There was no mistake, Mr. Lee." Lance stared hard at the florist as he returned to the front of the room. "He passed away sometime last night. Another inspector is on her way over here to secure the scene and help me start the investigation."

"But...how?" Finally, Lorelei found her voice. It was shaky and weak, but at least she could speak.

"We don't have any details right now." Lance had softened his voice. "Until we do, I need everyone to stay on the property. I want to get a statement from each of you."

Several people started to protest, but Lance silenced them all by holding up his hand.

"It's police procedure, and you don't have a choice. I apologize if that means you have to miss something, but it can't be helped."

Lorelei's soft voice spoke again from the sofa. "I don't believe it, either. I'm sure it's all a mistake. A terrible, horrible, awful mistake..."

Her words came faster and faster.

Uh-oh. I squeezed her knee tightly, but she didn't even acknowledge me. "Lorelei. Look at me. I need you to take a deep breath. C'mon. Breathe with me."

She slowly brought her gaze around to my face. By now, her shoulders were shaking and her skin looked unnaturally pale.

"She needs something to drink," I said loudly. "Something strong."

The young bride gazed at me helplessly, desperate for something, anything, to make sense of what she'd just heard.

"Get the woman something to drink," Lance repeated to the crowd. He quickly singled out Buck. "You, there. Get her something strong. Now!"

The best man sprang into action. He bolted from the sofa and made a beeline to a large globe that sat at the back of the room. With one yank, he opened the top half of the globe, which concealed a bar inside. Several bottles of liquor winked up from a black velvet lining. He reached for one, and then he poured about an inch's worth of alcohol into a tumbler, which he rushed back to the sofa. He'd obviously visited the bar before, since he knew exactly what to do.

"Here." He thrust the tumbler at Lorelei. "Drink this."

His hand shook as he passed her the drink.

Lorelei looked dubious, but she accepted his offering and downed it. Then she set the glass on the ground and closed her eyes. "I want to see him." Her voice was still shaky but audible. "Take me to him."

"I'm afraid I can't do that right now," Lance said. "We need to wait for the medical examiner first. She'll do an examination, and then I can let you see him."

"I'll stay with her." It was Nelle, who hadn't spoken until now. She moved around the sofa and elbowed me out of the way. "Lorelei, dear... come upstairs with me. You've had a terrible shock, and you need to lie down. I insist."

Although Lorelei tried to protest, her mother wouldn't take no for an answer. She gently took hold of her daughter's arm and carefully pulled her up from the couch. The minute she did that, Lorelei finally felt free enough to collapse into her mother's arms.

"There, there." Mrs. Honeycutt stroked her daughter's hair as the girl wept.

Lance turned to address the crowd. "Like I said...I need to get a statement from each of you. You can either go to your room or stay somewhere else, but please don't leave. I'd like you all to stay inside, too, until after the medical examiner leaves."

Given that directive, the group began to disband. It started with the lady in stilettos, whom I'd pegged for a maiden aunt the day before. She tottered out of the room, and she was followed by several others, including Buck, Jamie, and the bridesmaid from breakfast.

Darryl stayed behind, though. He cautiously approached Nelle, who stroked her daughter's hair. He stopped a few feet short of the sofa.

"Anything I can do?" he asked.

"No, I'm afraid not." Nelle continued to rake Lorelei's hair with her fingers. "Unless...could you please help me get Lorelei to her room?"

"Of course." Darryl positioned himself to the left of the bride and gently took hold of her elbow. The trio slowly tottered out of the sunroom and into the hall.

By now, everyone else had disappeared, except for Mr. Carmichael. He had crept from his chair to the open globe, where he stood, transfixed by the gleaming bottles.

"What now?" I whispered to Lance.

"Now we find out about the groom's family life." He nodded at Mr. Carmichael, who was filling a large tumbler with whiskey. "Ready or not, here we come."

Chapter 5

Not surprisingly, Mr. Carmichael looked shell-shocked. He stared at his drink, his eyes glassy and his expression vague.

"Mr. Carmichael?" Lance cautiously approached him, as if he was a wild animal that might bolt.

"Yes?" The man finally dredged his gaze away from the tumbler.

"Why don't you take a seat over there." Lance nodded to the small sofa, which had been getting more than its fair share of use this morning.

It wasn't a question, and he grudgingly moved to the wicker seat. As soon as he reached it, he practically fell onto the plaid cushion, the drink sloshing over the cup's side, while I perched on a nearby armchair. Only Lance stood, and he slowly withdraw a small notepad from his back pocket.

"I.,,I can't believe this has happened," Mr. Carmichael's voice was thick. "What…where…how?" He looked so pained, the creases on his forehead deepening with every word.

"It's okay." I leaned toward him. "Lance will explain everything."

"Thank you. Thank you, Miss…"

I was about to respond when something stopped me. His breath reeked of alcohol. He'd only had time to take a quick sip of his drink, so he must've arrived at the sunroom already tipsy.

My first instinct was to lean away. My second was to glance at Lance, who didn't notice my discomfort.

"That's Missy DuBois." Lance answered the man's question. "She went with the groundskeeper this morning to look for your son. Unfortunately, they found him, only it was at the bottom of a water tower."

"Oh, my God. Don't tell me he'd been beaten."

"No, that's not it." I quickly stole another glance at Lance. Of all the other things for someone to focus on, I didn't expect a beating to be the first one. "To be honest, it looked like he was only sleeping."

"Well, thank God for that." Mr. Carmichael sounded relieved. "I just knew something like this was going to happen to him. I warned that boy and warned that boy, but he wouldn't listen to me." He slowly drew his hand across his mouth, although it did nothing to staunch the smell. "How many times can you tell someone something before you finally give up?"

"What did you want him to stop, Mr. Carmichael?" Lance paused his notetaking to study the groom's father.

"Stop with the gambling, of course." Once again, his fingers trembled next to his mouth, just like Buck's had done when he gave Lorelei the drink.

"So, your son had a gambling problem?" Lance asked.

"Please call me Foster, and, yes, my son was addicted to gambling."

"That's too bad. What did he play?"

"You name it, he'd bet on it. It all started with fantasy football in law school. Apparently, Yale has quite an active fantasy football league. Wesley made a lot of money…at first. Enough that he thought about becoming a sports attorney when he graduated."

"Interesting," Lance said. "And did he? Go into that type of law, I mean."

"No, he didn't." Foster's expression darkened once more. "He never graduated, as a matter of fact. He lost everything at the racetrack in his last year at school. The tuition, his trust fund…all of it. A million dollars, right down the drain."

"Wow." My mind reeled. To think someone could blow through a million dollars in one year's time was mindboggling.

"Did your son gamble right up to his death?" Lance spoke quietly but firmly. He was a master at walking the fine line between being too direct and not direct enough.

"Well, I was hoping he'd quit. His mother seemed to think he did. Lorelei, too. She was so good to him. She still agreed to marry him, even when she found out what a mess he'd made of his life."

Which reminded me of something else. "I'm sorry, Mr. Carmichael, but I couldn't help but notice Lorelei's engagement ring yesterday. It's the biggest one I've ever seen. How in the world did Wesley manage to buy a five-carat diamond if he lost all his money?"

Normally, I wouldn't dream of asking such a personal question, but this was *not* a normal weekend. As far as I was concerned, all bets were off when it came to a police investigation, and I could—and often did—ask the most impolite questions.

"It was a family heirloom. My great-great-grandmother's. Since Wesley was my only son, he automatically got the ring."

"And you said his fiancée knew about his gambling problem?" Lance asked.

"She found out about a year ago. Of course, she wondered when he didn't take the Louisiana Bar Examination after law school, like his friends did. That was when he had to admit he never graduated."

"That's enough, Foster." A woman's shrill voice sliced the air.

We all turned at the sound. An older woman stood near the door to the sunroom, her arms folded tightly. It was the woman who'd fainted earlier, the one I'd assumed was Wesley's mother.

"He's going to find out anyway, Violet." Foster didn't even turn. He remained slumped in his seat, his gaze fixed straight ahead.

"It's our son you're talking about!" She hissed the words as she moved into the room. "Control yourself."

Lance studied the newcomer. "Your husband is helping the investigation by telling me what he knows, ma'am. It's important he give me as much information as possible."

"You'll have to get your information from someone else." She pulled up short of the sofa. She'd redone her hair, and the chignon looked perfectly coifed now. "I know how these things work. You're going to try and trip Foster up with your questions. Then he won't be able to take anything back. We are *not* saying another word until our attorney gets here."

"But that won't be necessary," Lance said. "I'm not accusing your husband of anything. I'm only soliciting his input into who may've killed your son."

"Violet—"

"Oh, no." She abruptly silenced her husband by wagging her finger at him. "I told you…I know how this works. We have the right to have an attorney present. It's the law."

"I can't make you talk to me, but you'll only be helping your son by telling me what you know."

"It doesn't work that way on TV," she said. "I want our attorney present, and I won't take no for an answer."

Finally, I couldn't take it any longer. This woman was impeding Lance's investigation and pretending to be an expert on something she knew nothing about.

"May I, Lance?" I whispered. When he quickly nodded, I rose from the armchair and moved closer to her. "This is an interview, Mrs. Carmichael. It's not an interrogation. Those are two separate things. Your husband hasn't been accused of a crime, and that's when the Miranda rights come into play. An interview is something completely different."

"But…but those television shows…"

"They don't represent reality. You don't need an attorney present every time a policeman questions you. Hollywood gets a lot of things wrong when it comes to police investigations."

Just when I thought she might change her mind, her jaw abruptly clenched.

"No. I won't do it. Come on, Foster." She turned to leave. "They can't keep you here against your will."

Foster looked miserable as he rose from the sofa. "I'm so sorry," he mumbled to Lance and me, before he followed his wife from the room.

My own jaw had begun to tense, so I took a deep breath. "Well, that was interesting. For a second, I thought she might change her mind."

"No…she's hiding something. But what?"

"I don't know, but I think her reaction was strange. She didn't react like a mother who'd just found out her son was killed."

"Agreed. I thought she'd be more surprised," I said.

"Then again, she did faint, so, it obviously came as a shock to her."

He fell silent for a moment. "Then again, she wasn't hyperventilating when I gave everyone the news. I was watching her husband, and I happened to catch her reaction. She was breathing normally."

"So you think she was acting?"

"Could be. Maybe she wasn't surprised by the news after all."

"She's a wonderful actress, then."

Already the morning had turned increasingly odd, and we'd only spoken to two people so far. Heaven only knew what the rest of the day would hold.

Chapter 6

There was so much to think about, a dull pain began to throb at the base of my skull. "I feel a headache coming on. I think I'll go rustle up an aspirin. I also want to tell Bo what happened with the *Riverboat Queen.*"

"Of course." Lance studied his notes one more time. "If you see the mother of the bride, please send her my way. I'd like to ask her what she knows about the groom's gambling problem."

"Sure." I slowly moved away from the sofa, the headache intensifying with every step.

By the time I reached the exit, though, I remembered something else. "By the way, Lance, did you notice the smell on Mr. Carmichael's breath? It was whiskey, and a lot of it. He'd been drinking before he got here."

"I thought I smelled something funny. At first I thought it came from the bar over there." Lance nodded at the open globe. "Nothing like a belt of whiskey before lunch, I guess."

"More like a bottle of it. See you later."

I gingerly stepped from the room. The hall was empty, since everyone else had headed upstairs to their bedrooms. The same was true for the foyer, which abutted another wing that was new to me. It was as if someone had thrown a heavy blanket over the house and cast a dull pall over everything underneath it.

That all changed when I arrived at the kitchen, though. I spied the back of a woman's dress, and it looked like Nelle Honeycutt. "Hello, there."

She immediately turned. "Hello, Missy."

"I'm so sorry about what's happened."

"Thank you, dear. I'm so sorry, too. Poor Lorelei. I don't know how she's ever going to recover from this."

"I'm sure she's very resilient. And she's young. I don't mean to sound flip, but she has a lot going for her."

"Of course, you're right, but it doesn't make it any easier, now does it? I just wish I could do something for her. Take away the pain. Maybe if I never..."

At that moment, a loud noise clattered at the front of the house.

"Hello? Is anyone home?" A woman's voice rang out, loud and clear.

"Oh, dear," Nelle said. "That would be Wesley's stepsister. Her plane was supposed to arrive at noon today."

I followed Nelle into the foyer. A tall, slim woman stood in the middle of it, and she had a mass of red curls that cascaded over pale, thin shoulders. She wore a sleeveless sundress and pink silk pumps, and she yelped when she spied Nelle.

"You must be Mrs. Honeycutt!" she shrieked. "It's fab-u-lous to finally meet you!"

She threw her arms around Nelle, the curls bouncing in every direction. "Thank you *sooo* much for hosting our family this weekend." She turned when she noticed me. "Are you a member of the family, too?"

"No, I'm not." I quickly thrust out my hand, since she looked ready to hug me next. "I'm a milliner. My name's Melissa DuBois, but everyone calls me Missy."

"Oh." The smile slipped from her face. "I thought you might be part of the family. That's too bad."

I tried not to take offense, which wasn't easy. "I didn't catch your name."

"I'm Electra Carmichael." She vigorously shook my hand. "Yes, it's a stage name. My real name is Lydia. But that's not very memorable, is it?"

That made sense, since I'd pegged her for an actress from the very beginning. "Nelle told me you're Wesley's sister."

"Stepsister," she quickly corrected. "His father married my mom. It'll make for some interesting seating arrangements at the wedding."

That caused both Nelle and me to flinch.

"About the wedding," I said. "Why don't we go into the sunroom?" No need to create a scene in the foyer. Not only that, but I wanted Lance to be the one to break the news to her, since it'd sound more official coming from a policeman.

"Okeydoke." She combed her fingers through her hair. "I'd love to freshen up a little, too. The plane ride from New York City was dreadful. Simply dreadful!" She rolled her eyes dramatically. "You have no idea what it's like to fly coach these days."

Little did she know, but I flew coach every time. "Bless your heart." I subtly guided her into the hall. "That must've been terrible."

When we reached the sunroom, I waited for her and Nelle to enter first so I could close the door behind us. Unfortunately, Lance was nowhere to be seen, so he must've left when I didn't return with Nelle right away. *Time for Plan B.*

"Can I get you something to drink?" Even though I'd judged Foster Carmichael harshly for drinking, I was about to give this girl some terrible news, so the least I could do was offer her a sip of something or other. Although it wasn't my bar—or my home—to offer, I didn't think Nelle would mind.

She didn't, because she nodded at me after I made the suggestion.

"How fun!" Electra's eyes lit up. "Sure, why not. This is a celebration. Do you have any champagne?"

I moved to the open globe and scanned its contents. Once I spotted a bottle of Dom Perignon, I pulled it from the velvet lining and set to work opening the cork. Meanwhile, Nelle guided Electra to a wingback chair by the sofa.

The girl happily flopped onto it and stretched out her legs. "Nice spread you have here, Mrs. Honeycutt."

"Please, call me Nelle. And thank you. It's been in my family for generations."

"This room reminds of a play I did back in New York," Electra said. "It was an Agatha Christie mystery. We all sat around on wicker furniture and tried to solve the case. It was terribly fun. We got horrible reviews, but what are you gonna do?"

I popped the bottle's cork and poured some into a flute. "Here you go." I crossed the room and placed the glass in her hand.

"Thank you, darling. Cheers!" She quickly gulped the champagne and dropped the empty glass to her lap. "So, where's Wesley?"

I took a deep breath, since there was no easy way to break the news. "There's been a terrible accident, I'm afraid."

I chose my words carefully. While I didn't know whether Wesley's death was accidental or not, it sounded better than to say he'd been murdered. Time would only tell if foul play was involved.

"Accident? Is that why there's a white van outside that says 'medical examiner'?"

"Yes," I said. "I'm afraid we had to call her. It's Wesley. We found his body this morning in a water tower."

"Wha...? What do you mean?" She jerked forward, her eyes wide. "That's not possible. Wesley knows how to swim. He's an excellent swimmer."

"No, no. That's not it. He didn't drown. But he did pass away. I'm sorry to have to be the one to tell you that."

"No...I don't believe you." She jumped up, which sent the champagne flute crashing to the ground. "You must be wrong. I don't know what's going on, but if this is some kind of sick joke, it's not funny!"

Joke? "No. Of course not. It's not a joke." I raised my hands in protest. "Trust me, I would never do that. I'm afraid your stepbrother passed away."

She wavered for a split second, before she fell back into the chair. "Oh, my God. This is terrible. Dreadful. Poor Wesley!"

"There, there." Nelle finally joined the conversation. "We know this is a terrible shock. It's the last thing anyone expected."

"But I should've been there." The girl looked horrified now. "What will people think of me? They'll want to know why I wasn't there when it happened. I was stuck on that god-awful plane...that's where I was."

That caught my attention. The girl in front of me had just found out about her stepbrother's death, but her first thought was for herself? Maybe it was the way she processed grief, but it sounded terribly self-centered.

"Were you two close, then?" I asked.

"Well, not really. To be honest, I haven't seen him in ten years. But that doesn't mean I don't care."

"No, of course not. I'm sure you two had your reasons."

"I was in New York, you see." She sounded anxious now to explain herself. "And he was working here, in his law practice. I couldn't exactly afford to fly all over the country."

I didn't have the heart to correct her. According to Foster Carmichael, Wesley didn't practice law anywhere. *Strange she doesn't know that.* Even if they hadn't spoken in years, I would think she'd at least have asked him about his occupation.

Slowly, she brushed her hair away from her cheek, which was bone dry. Sunlight dappled her face and highlighted her sharp cheekbones and arched eyebrows.

"Oh, the way to dusty death!" she suddenly cried. "Life is but a walking shadow." Her face remained tilted to the sun, which was streaming through the window.

"Wait a minute. Isn't that the speech from *Macbeth*?" I'd performed the play while a student at Vanderbilt, and I seemed to recall Macbeth said those words after his wife committed suicide.

"Why, yes." Her head snapped down again. "You have a good ear for dialogue. Most people can't place those lines."

Before I could say more, my cell jingled in my pocket, and I quickly withdrew it. To be honest, I welcomed a little relief from Electra's theatrics. "I'm sorry," I said. "But I should take this call."

By now, I realized it was Ambrose calling me, and I silently praised him for his excellent timing.

"Of course. After all, 'To thine own self be true.'"

I quickly took my leave, the sound of her voice trailing behind me. Apparently, Electra wanted to perform the rest of Macbeth's soliloquy for Nelle, and she quickly launched into the next line. *Bless her heart.*

The moment I accepted Ambrose's call, I heard his voice on the other end of the line.

"Hey there, darlin'."

All at once, my shoulders began to relax. Leave it to Bo to calm me down with a single sentence. "Gosh, I wish you were here."

"I wish I was there, too. How are things going?"

"Not so good." I quickly told Bo about the morning's grisly turn of events. "Lance had to tell the family we found Wesley's body. They were all devastated, of course."

"Of course. Do you want me to meet you there?"

Sweet of him to ask. "No, there's really nothing you can do. Turns out Wesley Carmichael had a gambling problem, so now Lance suspects murder. The medical examiner is out there with his body."

"Well, that's good. Although, I still think I should drive out there. I don't want you to have to face this all on your own."

"It's okay, really. It's not my first murder investigation. Remember?"

Unfortunately, I'd had similar conversations with Bo in the past. Ever since someone died at Morningside Plantation, I'd run across several other murders in my travels. Not that I wanted, or needed, the drama in my life, but that was the way things had happened ever since I moved to Bleu Bayou.

"I know," he said. "That seems like a lifetime ago. You've been involved in four cases since then."

"Five. But who's counting? Only this one is different. People have been reacting in such strange ways. The victim's parents won't even talk to Lance—at least his stepmother won't—and his stepsister started quoting Shakespeare when I told her about the death."

"That *is* weird. How's the bride holding up?"

"I don't know. I haven't seen her in a while. But I spoke with her mom, and I think everyone's pretty much in a fog at this point."

Speaking of which...I still hadn't sent Nelle over to meet with Lance.
"Look, Ambrose. I have to go. I promised Lance I'd help him with
something."

"Okay. I won't keep you then, but there's something else you should
know. Something's happened over here."

Uh-oh. Little by little, my shoulders began to tense again. The last thing
I needed was more bad news. "What do you mean?"

"It's about our wedding."

"Our wedding?" Now I knew I was cursed. I'd already taken a call from
Brandy d'Aulnay that morning, which I never did tell Bo about. "That
reminds me...I meant to tell you something, too. One of the d'Aulnay
sisters called me this morning."

"D'Aulnay? Isn't that the name of the family that owns the *Riverboat
Queen*?"

"It is, and Brandy's one of the daughters. She said the boat caught fire
last night and the kitchen burned."

"That's terrible. Will they be able to fix it in time?"

"No, they can't," I said. "We have to find another venue. Can you
believe it?"

When he didn't answer me for a few seconds, I worried we might've
been disconnected. "Bo...are you still there?"

"Yeah, I'm here. Well, that's too bad. Why don't we talk about it when
you get home tonight?"

"Okay. But what did you want to tell me?" I detected some hesitation
in his voice. He was hiding something, and now he couldn't wait to get
off the phone.

"It's not important. I'll tell you tonight. You've got enough going on
right now."

"Ambrose Jackson." While I appreciated his concern, I didn't like where
this conversation was heading. If he had more news, I needed to hear it,
whether I wanted to or not. "Please tell me what's happened."

"Okay. But are you sitting down?"

"No, I'm standing. Does it matter?"

"It might. I found out something about our wedding photographer."

"Okay. Let me have it."

"I was working with a client," he said, "and she told me all about her
wedding plans."

"And?"

"And she's the daughter of a pretty famous senator. It's Senator Rios,
out of the Valley."

"Well, good for her." That didn't sound like bad news at all. "And good for you, too." The senator was one of the most important politicians in Louisiana, so the job would bring Bo tons of publicity. Although I honestly had no idea how it would affect our wedding.

"Well, we had our first appointment today," he said.

"Could you please tell me the news?" At this rate, I was never going to find out what had happened.

"Now, don't get mad, but she's using the same photographer we are."

"Why would I be mad about that?" I'd hired a photographer named Dana to shoot our wedding, and she owned a studio near mine. We often ran into each other by the elevator to the atrium. "She can shoot any weddings she wants to. It's a free country."

"Yeah, but the wedding is the same date as ours." He abruptly cleared his throat. "At the same time."

"Excuse me?" Surely I misunderstood. With all the hullaballoo this morning, my mind must be playing tricks on me.

"She's getting married the same day as we are," he repeated. "At the same time."

"But...but that's impossible. How can a photographer be in two places at once? You must have heard her wrong."

"I'm afraid I didn't. Turns out the senator's staff booked the photographer only a week ago. She must've said yes without realizing she's shooting our wedding that day."

"That's...that's awful! She'll never turn down the chance to shoot a high-profile wedding like that. She's going to cancel on us. I just know it!"

"Okay, now calm down." Once again, Ambrose cleared his throat. He seemed to buying time so I could rein in my emotions. He always did that when it sounded like I was ready to jump off the nearest ledge. "She hasn't called you yet, right? Maybe she's going to come up with a plan."

"A plan? Like how to split herself in two?"

"Maybe she's going to have her assistant shoot our wedding. Or the other way around."

"Think about it, Bo. She's not going to palm off the senator's daughter to an assistant. If anything, she'll give us the B team and shoot the other wedding herself."

"We don't know that yet," he said. "Why don't we give her the benefit of the doubt until we hear from her?"

Leave it to Bo to be calm, cool, and collected, while I wanted to throw something out the nearest window. "You don't sound upset about this, Bo. Why aren't you more upset?"

"Because you're upset enough for both of us," he said. "Plus, it's not the ceremony I care about. It's you. I could marry you in a pizza parlor and still be happy."

That took the fight right out of me. "Awww." Of all the nice things to say—and he'd said many over the years—that one took the cake. "You're right. You always mange to keep things in perspective."

"Someone has to," he teased. "Look, just do what you have to do over there and then hurry home. We'll figure this out."

With that, he blew me a kiss—the squeak of his smooch tickled my ear—and hung up the phone. It took a moment for me to realize he was gone. I still couldn't process the idea of losing our photographer to someone else. Even someone more famous and with much better connections.

It seemed the universe was conspiring against us, and we had only four weeks to go until our ceremony.

Chapter 7

I finally lowered the phone and turned around. While I expected to find Nelle and Electra in the same place where I left them, they'd disappeared. The only reminder of our talk was an overturned champagne flute on the floor.

I'd missed the chance to tell Nelle about Lance. So I left the room as well, anxious to find her and send her to Lance. If I couldn't do that, at least I could tell Lance about our conversation with Electra.

Silence engulfed me again as I moved through the hall. Gone was the laughter that characterized the morning; the happy chitchat and excited hubbub. It gave way to an oppressive quiet that had me tiptoeing all the way to the foyer. If people were out and about this morning, I couldn't see them, and it stayed that way until I reached the front room.

Finally, I spied someone standing by the entrance. "Hi, Darryl."

He quickly turned, but his face looked troubled.

"Is something wrong?"

He indicated a package in his hand. It was a gift-wrapped box, covered in shiny silver paper and tied with a velvet bow.

"Well, that's pretty. Who's it from?"

"I don' know," he finally said. "Someone done sent it ta dat boy."

"Wesley?" I glanced down and noticed the gift came with no card. Someone had scrawled Wesley's name on the wrapping but forgot to include a note. "I wonder who it's from?"

"I gots no idea," he said.

"Maybe you should give it to the bride, then. But you might want to wait a little. She probably doesn't want to see anything like that right now."

"It's not fer her." Darryl eyed the package protectively. "Someone wants it ta reach da boy."

"Then why don't you give it to Lance? He'll know what to do with it." As a matter of fact, I intended to find Lance myself, so maybe I could spare Darryl the trouble. "Or you can just hand it over to me. I need to speak with Lance anyway."

"Okay, den." Darryl shrugged and gave me the box.

It was heavy, and about the size of a toaster. I cradled it in my arms as I stepped past him and moved away from the foyer.

The shiny silver paper winked at me as I walked. Someone had gone to a lot of trouble to wrap the package, but why didn't he or she include a gift tag? I mulled that over as I walked, and before long, I arrived at the kitchen.

Lance stood near it, with his head bent low over his notebook.

"Hey there, Lance."

He glanced up from his notes. "I thought you were going to find the mother-of-the-bride for me."

"I was, but she slipped away before I could do that. Look at this."

He eyed the package curiously. "What is it?"

"I have no idea." I walked into the kitchen and laid it on the counter. "And I met Wesley Carmichael's stepsister. I need to tell you about her. She was a real piece of work."

"First things first." Lance sidled up to the counter, too. "Where'd you get the gift?"

"Darryl handed it to me. It's for Wesley."

"Wesley?" Lance said. "That's strange. People don't usually send a gift to the groom."

"Tell me about it. They usually send one to the bride's home, or maybe they bring it to the reception."

"There's only one way to find out what's in it." Lance quickly took a pair of latex gloves from his back pocket, which he slipped over his fingers. Then he reached for the box and carefully peeled away the first layer of wrapping paper. After working his way through another layer, he unearthed a brown cardboard box sealed with strapping tape. He carefully stored the paper to one side, before he slowly peeled off the tape and opened the lid.

We both peered into the box at the same time.

"It's a clock." I quickly appraised the rich brown case with an elaborately scrolled base. "A beautiful clock. Why would someone send a clock to a guy on his wedding day?"

"Beats me." Lance withdrew the clock from the box and balanced it in his hands.

The mantel clock was probably a hundred years old. The case was mahogany, like I'd thought, and a rim of gold circled the dial. Someone had removed the pendulum, and the hands pointed to six and twelve.

"What a beauty." The details were extraordinary, including the latticework base and four filigreed feet that supported it. "It looks expensive."

"Hm, mmm." Lance angled the clock to the window, where it glowed in the noontime sun.

Once he finished inspecting the front of the clock, he slowly turned it over and inspected the back. All at once, he let out a long, low whistle. "Well, look at that."

I glanced over his shoulder. Across the back of the clock, someone had scrawled a few words in black felt pen. The letters singed the wood like a lightning strike: Time's Up.

Lance and I gaped at each other.

"Who would do that?" I finally asked. "They've ruined it."

"I want to know *why* they did it. That's an even better question."

"Someone obviously had it in for Wesley." I noticed the writing was scratchy and raw, since the back was covered in pine, instead of expensive mahogany, like the front.

"I need to get this to the lab to be fingerprinted." Lance gently placed the clock back in its carrying case. "Then again…" his voice trailed off as he studied it.

"What?" I never knew what to expect with Lance. He often surprised me with how he handled evidence.

"I might just hold off on sending this to the station. It'd be interesting to see what people around here think about this little present."

"Oh, I get it. You want to see if maybe someone in the wedding party sent it."

"Bingo. It's hard for people to deny something when you put the evidence right in front of them."

Something rustled behind us just then, and we both turned. A medical examiner bustled into the kitchen wearing a white lab coat with a logo for the St. James Parish Medical Examiner's Office stitched onto the pocket. Since St. James was only one parish over, I guessed it shared its employees with the parish where the wedding was to take place.

"Hello, Adaline."

"Missy! Good to see you again."

"You two know each other?" Lance looked surprised.

"Of course I know Missy," Adaline said. "We've worked together several times."

Since even the medical examiner knew my name, odds were good I had a penchant for finding dead bodies. But that was neither here nor there at the moment.

"I hope you've been well since our last visit." The last time we spoke, Adaline had a bad case of shingles that nearly landed her in the hospital.

"I'm much better now." Her eyebrows suddenly shot up. "Wait a minute. Don't tell me you're the one who found the body this time, too?"

"Guilty as charged. The house's caretaker and I went looking for the groom when he didn't show up at breakfast this morning."

"There was no chance of that," she said. "The victim died last night."

She must've concluded her initial investigation, which she would type up and present to Lance as an official report.

"Anything else you can tell us about the body?" Lance asked.

"You'll get a preliminary later today. I'll rush it." She raked her fingers through her short, gray hair, some of which was plastered to her forehead by sweat. "It's like a furnace out there. Not a very good day for a murder investigation, is it?"

"Did you say, 'murder'?" Lance shot her a funny look.

"Oh, yeah. I found a second pair of footprints in some mud near the body. Too large for the victim's, so it had to be someone else's."

My mind immediately flew back to my time with Darryl. Since he'd bent over the body to determine whether Wesley was still breathing or not, his rubber boots could've left prints in the mud. "Say, Adaline. Did the prints have smooth soles, or rough?"

"They looked smooth," she said. "No indentations. Why?"

"Because I thought they might belong to the caretaker. He was with me when we found the body. But his boots had treads on the bottom."

"Then they're not his prints," she said, matter-of-factly. "These prints were smooth as a baby's bottom."

"Let me get this straight," Lance slowly crossed his arms. "There's no way the man's death was an accident, then?"

"None at all. Someone either killed him in the tower or brought him there afterward. Either way, there was another person involved."

I knew why Lance had asked. Up until now, we could all pretend that maybe Wesley's death didn't involve foul play. There was no chance of that now, though.

"Another person was involved in what?"

A woman spoke up behind us, and her voice sounded shaky and weak.

I turned to see Lorelei standing in the entrance to the kitchen. A messy ponytail splayed over one shoulder, thick and matted, and her eyes looked glassy. It seemed she'd just gotten out of bed, or maybe she needed to be there.

"Ummm..." Even Lance didn't know what to say.

"Well? Aren't you going to tell me?"

Finally, Lance regained his composure. "We have some bad news about your fiancé. About how he died."

"Oh? I thought it was an accident, right?"

The medical examiner started to say something, but Lance silenced her by raising his hand.

"First of all. I think you should meet someone. This is Adaline Clark, with the St. James Parish Medical Examiner's Office."

"Thank goodness." Lorelei breathed a huge sigh of relief. "I'm so glad you're here. People are saying all kinds of terrible things about Wesley. Like how maybe he didn't hit his head and fall down. Like how maybe someone killed him."

She shook her head and the ponytail flew forward. "But I don't think that's what happened. My poor Wesley obviously took too much medicine and got confused. He probably hit his head, or maybe he fell down on the pavement. I just hope he went quickly and it wasn't too painful."

She gazed at Lance hopefully, waiting for him to agree with her.

"Well, I'm afraid that's *not* how it happened." Lance spoke gently, but firmly. "There's no easy way to say this. Someone was with your fiancé when he died, so now we suspect foul play."

"But...but that doesn't mean anything," she sputtered. "Maybe one of his buddies was there and the guy tried to help him after Wesley fell. Maybe he tried to get help. Did you ever think of that, Officer?" She was grasping at straws, and we all knew it.

"Miss Honeycutt." Up until this point, Adaline had held her tongue. "I won't have an official report until later this afternoon, but I can tell you this—off the record—that someone poisoned your fiancé. I noticed bubbling on the surface of his skin."

"Poison?" That took the fight right out of Lorelei. "But...but I don't know how that could be."

"Did Wesley have any enemies you know of?" Lance asked.

"I...I guess so. I mean, doesn't everyone?"

"I'm not talking about little squabbles." Lance's voice reminded firm. "I mean, did he upset someone to the point they may have wanted to kill him?"

Before she could respond, another noise reached us. But this one was loud and chaotic. Something metal crashed to the ground in the foyer, and it was followed by a string of very colorful curses.

"Could you please see what's happening out there?" Lance asked me.

"Of course." It was the least I could do, since he obviously wanted to speak more with Lorelei.

I practically flew into the foyer, hoping to silence the noisemaker. When I arrived, I skidded to a stop, since I encountered the last person I expected to see: Stormie Lanai, the newscaster. And she looked none too happy to see me, either.

Chapter 8

"It's you!" I didn't mean to yell, but she'd surprised the heck out of me.

"Of course, it's me. We were trying to film out here, but my cameraman broke the camera lens."

A cameraman crouched on the ground behind Stormie, holding a busted lens. The rest of his equipment was scattered on the floor, as if he'd dropped it in a panic. "The station manager isn't going to like this. Not one bit."

Stormie scowled at him. "Then fix it. We still have to shoot some footage."

"Don't tell me you're going through with the story?" I asked. "Haven't you heard about the body we found on the property?"

"Yes, I have. But that doesn't mean my job here is done." She fluttered her false eyelashes, which always reminded me of two butterflies about to take flight. "It only means I'll be working on a different kind of story now. Real news…not the fluffy wedding piece my editor wanted me to cover."

Heaven forbid Lorelei should wander into the foyer and find a news crew waiting for her, so I had to get rid of them.

"I'm sorry, but you have to leave. The police detective is talking to the bride in the kitchen."

"He is?" She glanced over my shoulder. "Why didn't you say so? That'll make for some excellent footage!"

"Oh no you don't." I blocked her with my shoulders. "Don't you dare go anywhere near Lorelei."

"Last I checked, this wasn't your house."

"No, but it is *my* house," someone new said.

Sure enough, I turned to see Nelle standing behind us. "And I'll thank you to get out of here."

The newscaster's demeanor immediately changed. She rushed to Nelle's side, the picture of concern now. "I'm so sorry about what happened. What a horrible thing to face on your daughter's wedding day! Is there anything I can do to help?"

I rolled my eyes. If I knew Stormie—which I did—the last thing she wanted was to help someone else. More likely, she wanted to help herself get a story that was guaranteed to lead off the nightly news.

"Come off it, Stormie," I said. "We all know why you're here. You want to get the scoop on this story before someone else beats you to it."

Her eyelids fluttered even faster. "That's a terrible thing to say! Even coming from you. I only want to help the family in its time of need."

"Do you, really?" Nelle sounded equally suspicious. "The best thing you can do is leave. Please take your cameraman and your tripod and whatever else you brought, and get off the property."

"But…but we already have such wonderful footage of the mansion!" Stormie gestured to the camcorder on the ground. "Would you like to see it?"

The offer came as a complete surprise. Especially since the cameraman seemed more concerned with his broken lens than with us.

"I'd be happy to share it with you." Stormie reached for the camcorder, before she seemed to remember something. "Charles? Could you please be a dear and help me lift the equipment?"

She turned to Nelle as the cameraman hoisted the equipment onto his knee.

"My doctor doesn't want me lifting anything over five pounds." She whispered the news, as if she was sharing an important secret. "It's bad for the baby, you know."

"A baby?" Nelle's tone abruptly softened. "Why didn't you say so? I never would've yelled at you like that if I knew you were with child. Dear me, that was just awful of me."

"No, no." Stormie waved casually, as if she hadn't given it another thought. "I didn't take offense. You had no way of knowing."

"Now you, on the other hand…" She gave me a pointed look, as if I should've volunteered to lift the camcorder for her.

"It's under the weight limit," I said, as innocently as I could. "Those things only weigh three or four pounds nowadays, so your doctor wouldn't mind."

Gracious light. At this rate, I wouldn't be surprised if Stormie stretched out the pregnancy to a year or two, instead of the usual nine months, so she could guilt people into lifting things for her.

"Yes, well, you can never be too careful." She turned her attention back to her number one priority...Nelle.

"We got some wonderful shots of your property." She leaned across the cameraman and angled the viewfinder out. "The house's colors look just gorgeous! It was made for the camera. Even the flowers look great, especially the magnolias. We took footage over by the garden, inside the family chapel, and near the pull-through drive. We have some terrific B-roll."

To be honest, something about the footage intrigued me, as well. I wondered if Lance knew about it and whether he could use it in his investigation.

"May I see the footage, too?" I took a step closer.

"Suit yourself." Stormie pushed the start button, and scenes began to scroll by on the viewfinder. It played everything from panoramic shots of rice fields outside the fence line to close-ups of magnolia blossoms. At one point, the images switched to a long, panoramic view of the exterior, from one end of the property to the other.

My breath stalled when the camera alighted on the stairwell by the wine cellar. "Stop the memory card!" I gasped.

"What?" Stormie seemed annoyed at the interruption. "Why?"

"When did you take this?" I continued to watch the scene, mesmerized.

"I don't know. About eleven this morning. Maybe eleven thirty. Does it really matter?"

"Yes. Stop the card. And please rewind it back a few seconds."

Fortunately, Stormie listened to me this time, and she reluctantly hit the pause button. Then she pushed rewind, and the card reversed itself.

"Okay, fine," she said. "You don't have to yell. Geesh...what's your problem?"

"There." I jabbed my finger at the viewfinder, once the card went back to a particular spot. "That's what I'm talking about."

Framed within the viewfinder was a shot of the stairs that led down to the wine cellar. The statue at the top of the stairs, which Lance had replaced after our visit there, was gone. It had completely disappeared, with nothing but a bit of leftover debris on the ground to show for it.

"When did you say you shot this?" I asked.

"About eleven." Stormie shrugged. "I still don't see why it matters."

I turned around, instead of answering her. Now I was eager to get back to the kitchen and find Lance. I flew down the hall and arrived there before either Stormie or Nelle could move.

Once I skidded into the kitchen, I hurried to Lance's side. "You need to come with me."

He seemed to be finishing up with Lorelei, and he didn't look happy I'd interrupted him. "Are you sure? We're almost done here."

"I'm afraid so," I said. "There's something important you need to see outside."

I moved next to Lorelei. "I'm sorry, but I need to take Detective LaPorte away for a little bit. Your mother's down the hall, in the foyer. Would you like me to send her in here?"

She sniffled and shook her head. "No thanks. She doesn't know I left my room. I think I'll just go upstairs and lie down again."

Once I realized she was going to be all right, I grabbed Lance's hand and practically pulled him from the kitchen. The noontime heat was almost unbearable when we stepped outside, and humidity clung to me like wet cotton. Once again, I thanked my lucky stars I'd opted to wear ballet flats today, because we cut across the lawn at breakneck speed.

After a moment, we arrived at the stairwell that led to the wine cellar.

"Look." I pointed at the empty landing.

"What happened to the statue?"

"I don't know. But I'm afraid we're going to find out."

I took the stairs two at a time, until I arrived at the doorway. Bravery was one thing, but foolhardiness was quite another, so I waited for Lance to enter the wine cellar first. He was the one who carried a sidearm in his waistband, not me, and I had no idea what awaited us.

The air in the cellar was much cooler than the air outside. Almost at once, the humidity on my skin and hair began to evaporate, and my eyes adjusted to the dim light. I automatically reached for the light switch on the wall, and pale, gold light flooded the space as soon as I flicked it on.

"Cross your fingers we're not too late," Lance said.

Once the shadows disappeared, I sized up the room. It looked exactly the same as before. Over there was the bar with the elaborate monogram carved on its side. A line of casks stairstepped up the opposite wall, and each was branded with the same monogram. Even the barstools looked untouched, with their seats swiveled to face the same direction. But that wasn't what we were looking for.

We made our way to a certain shelf on the wall, and when we reached it, I loudly gasped. "Sassafras! They're gone."

Sure enough, the wineglasses Lance planned to "bag and tag" later for evidence, once he'd had a chance to measure their position on the shelf, had disappeared.

"Holy cow." He spoke behind me. "That's what I was afraid of. I should've taken them when I had the chance."

"But you had no idea they were going to disappear."

"At least I still have this."

He slowly reached behind his back and withdrew a shiny plastic bag from his pocket. Inside was the cigarette paper we'd found on the floor. It looked so innocent lying in a sheath of plastic: just another rectangular slip of white paper with crisp edges and clean sides.

"That's right!" I eyed the bag. "At least they didn't get that, did they?"

"Nope." He returned the evidence to his pocket. "Look, I'm going to seal up this room more tightly, so no one else can come down here. It's too late for the wineglasses, but there could be some other evidence we haven't seen. Do you mind checking on the bride while I do that?"

"No, of course not. She said she was going back to her room, so I'll check there first."

"Stay in touch. And keep your eyes open. I have a feeling we've already crossed paths with our killer."

I gulped. "That's a creepy way to put it."

"I know, but it's the truth. Be careful."

I left the room and quickly climbed the stairs. Once more, humidity settled over my head and shoulders the minute I emerged from the cool stairwell, and it only got worse as I made my way toward the mansion.

I was so engrossed in my thoughts—Why would someone take the wineglasses? Who else knew about the wine cellar?—that I barely noticed someone on the path ahead of me. In fact, I didn't notice him until we nearly collided, and our heads jerked up at the same time.

"Whoa!" I said.

It was Buck Liddell, the best man I'd met in the sunroom. He'd seemed so casual about everything before, but now he moved like the wind. Wherever he was headed, he couldn't get there fast enough.

"Sorry about that." He held his cell phone in one hand and a brand-new Samsonite in the other. "I'm trying to get an Uber, and I didn't see you."

"I could tell that. You're Buck Liddell, right?"

He squinted at me. "Yeah, I am. And you're that girl who was helping the police detective."

"Yes. I'm Missy DuBois. Were you going somewhere?"

It was hard to miss the suitcase, or the crisp linen blazer he'd donned since I last saw him.

"There's been an emergency at my dad's business." He slowly moved the suitcase behind his back, as if I wouldn't notice it then. "He asked me to come to New Orleans to help him out this afternoon."

"But you can't leave." Strange he didn't remember how Lance specifically told everyone in the wedding party to stay put. "The detective wants to interview everyone who was supposed to be in the wedding tonight."

"I already told him what I know. Staying here isn't going to help anyone out, and my father really needs me. He told me the store's packed with tourists and two of his best salespeople called in sick."

"That may be, but I'm afraid you still can't leave." If anything, I was more determined than ever to keep him from disobeying Lance's orders. *Who does he think he is?* "Detective LaPorte wants everyone to stay on the property. Including you."

"Now look here." He set the suitcase on the ground, clearly frustrated. "I don't know who made you the watchdog around here, but I'll only be gone for one afternoon. I plan to come right back after the store closes for the night."

"Then what's with the suitcase?"

"It's none of your business. I don't owe you an explanation for anything."

I brought my hand to my pocket and quickly withdrew my cell. While I hated to play hardball with Buck, he'd left me no choice. "Why don't we get the detective on the phone, then, and see what he says?"

"For the love of God." He picked up the suitcase again. "Fine. I'll stay here. Just like a prisoner. 'The Prisoner of Honeycutt Hall.' It sounds like a bad horror flick."

He swiveled around, and the minute he did that, the suitcase burst open. A blur of books and knickknacks flew in every direction. Some of it landed on the grass, while most of it rolled under the beautyberry bush.

"Now look what you've done!" He glared at me.

"Me? You're the one who huffed out of here."

I bent to help him, although he quickly tried to scoop everything up before I could. I spied an antique textbook under the hedge, which I bent to retrieve. The minute I straightened, I spied something else amid the bush's thorny roots. It was long and shiny, and about as round as a rolling pin.

I lunged for it with my left hand, since the textbook weighted down my other one. It was a candlestick, of all things. A beautiful silver candlestick, burnished with age, and inscribed with the distinctive HH logo on its side.

"What's this?" I brought the candlestick into the sunlight.

"That's just something Mrs. Honeycutt wanted me to appraise." He held out his hand for it. "Here. I'll see if there's any damage."

"Not so fast." I pulled the candlestick out of his reach. "It looks like you were hiding it in your bag."

"Hiding it?" he scoffed. "That's ridiculous. I told you...Mrs. Honeycutt wanted an appraisal. My father owns an antiques store in the French quarter, and I work there with him. She's having everything appraised, for some reason."

"I see." I began to hand over the candlestick and the book when I spied something else winking up at me from the ground. It, too, was shiny, although the hedge obscured most of it.

I reached for it before Buck could stop me. Chunks of bark mulch dusted the surface, which I brushed aside to unearth an exquisite picture frame, inlaid with rows of semiprecious stones. Amethysts, jade, pearls... the stones glinted prettily in the sunlight. "My gosh. This is gorgeous!"

Buck grabbed it from me. "It's been in the Honeycutt family since the Civil War. Someone buried it in the backyard for safekeeping, and no one knew it was there until last year."

"Let me guess...it's something else Mrs. Honeycutt wanted you to appraise?" While I could believe his explanation for the silver candlestick, the frame seemed terribly expensive to be thrown into a suitcase like that.

"Yes. She asked me to take it back to the store."

"Look, Buck. All of this seems pretty incredible. Think about it: you're calling for a car, you have a suitcase stuffed with things from the mansion, and, between you and me, you can't wait to get out of here. What am I supposed to think?"

He hemmed and hawed a bit, probably trying to think of a plausible explanation. "If you don't believe me, ask Mrs. Honeycutt. She'll tell you it's true."

"Just in case...do you mind if I hold onto those things in the meantime? You told me you weren't going to go anywhere, and I'd feel better if I got them back to Nelle myself."

He gave an exaggerated sigh. "You're really being difficult, you know that? But if you insist." He threw up his hands.

"I do."

"You're going to feel like a fool when she backs up my story. She'll tell you I'm legit. And when she does, I expect a full-blown apology."

"And you'll get it. Just as soon as your story checks out." I handed him the textbook, but I kept the candlestick and the picture frame firmly in my grasp. Buck had no choice but to beat a hasty retreat with his much lighter suitcase, which trailed behind him.

I watched him turn and walk away from me, so much slower than when he first barreled down the path. After everything that had happened just now, it was time to catch my breath and have a good, long chat with Lance. Maybe Buck was the one Lance warned me about, and I didn't even realize it at the time.

Chapter 9

By the time I turned around and headed for the wine cellar, Lance had already left. Electric-yellow caution tape stretched along the top of the stairwell, and a Master Lock padlock secured the door at the very bottom.

I thought about calling Lance on my cell. But then I realized I might as well head for the main house, since no one else seemed to be outside anyway. If I couldn't find Lance, I could always look for Nelle, since I was dying to know whether Buck was telling the truth about the antiques.

This time, I watched where I was walking as I headed up the path. After a moment, I passed a large holly tree, and something rustled loudly on the other side. It piqued my curiously, and I paused long enough to determine the source of the sound.

Apparently, two people stood on the other side of the bush. Their voices drifted through the branches, just loud enough for me to hear.

"I thought you'd still be hiding in your room." The speaker was Violet, Wesley's mother. She sounded dubious, as if she never expected to find her companion away from the house.

"I wasn't 'hiding' anywhere." The second voice belonged to Lorelei, of all people. Unlike before, when she turned soft-spoken and weepy after she heard the details of Wesley's death, she sounded revived now. As if she'd mustered the strength to get through the terrible weekend, by whatever means necessary.

Thankfully, the holly bush was immense—one of those Nellie Stevens Hollies—and it provided more than enough foliage to keep me covered. I settled back on my heels and waited for Violet to respond.

"Well, that's what it seemed like to me," Violet said.

"I don't necessarily care what you think." Lorelei clipped the ends of her words, her anger barely concealed.

"Now that you're here, though," Violet continued, "I need to talk to you about something. About the ring Wesley gave you. It belonged to Foster's great-great-grandmother, you know."

"The ring? You want to talk to me about the engagement ring?" Lorelei seemed incredulous.

To be fair, it seemed awfully sudden for Violet to bring up the poor girl's engagement ring. She only learned about his death a little while ago, and the ring wasn't exactly going anywhere. Surely, Violet could wait.

The older woman's voice brought me back to the present. "He never asked us if he could give it to you, you know. We always thought he'd wait a little longer before he got married."

"He said the ring belonged to him. He said it was his to give away." Lorelei's voice had hardened, as well. Apparently, there was no love lost between Wesley's fiancée and his mother.

I decided to lean a little closer to the conversation. The minute I did that, though, something pricked me on the arm, and I flinched.

Sweet mother of pearl!

The jagged edges of a leaf scraped against my skin and left an angry red mark. Although the Nellie Stevens Holly wouldn't sprout berries until later, the edges of its waxy green leaves were shaped like needles. So I nursed my arm while I tried to remain silent.

"What's the use?" Lorelei sounded resigned now. "Here. Take it. I don't want it anyway."

I carefully pried apart a branch in front of me, careful to avoid the needle-sharp edges this time, and saw two women on the other side. Lorelei stood with her back to me, and, just as I thought, she held the ring out to Violet. The older woman hesitated, but then she reached to pluck it from Lorelei's hand.

Before she could grab it, though, Lorelei released the ring.

"Oops! Clumsy me."

Violet's eyes widened as she watched the ring fall to the ground, where it landed in the dust. Even from where I stood, the diamond glittered in the sun, like a drop of water splashed on the earth.

"How could you?!" Violet shrieked. "You...you brat! Pick the ring up right now."

"Make me." Lorelei jutted out her chin, daring Violet to move.

"Why...why." Violet seemed caught between a rock and a hard place. Between wanting to teach Lorelei a lesson and wanting to get her heirloom off the dusty ground. It was a no-win situation, since neither party looked willing to back down.

Now, I had been privy to some nasty conversations in my day—after all, I worked in the bridal business, where I'd seen more than my share of bridezillas—but this one seemed particularly harsh. These two women supposedly loved Wesley, so why couldn't they get along?

"Excuse me." I skirted around the bush until I stood in the open. "Is there a problem?"

Neither woman expected to see me, and neither one answered.

"I was just walking around the grounds, and I thought I heard something." When in doubt, it's best to pretend you're an innocent bystander, I'd found. That way people think you never intended to eavesdrop, so they're not offended.

"We were having a private conversation." Violet spoke a bit more harshly than necessary.

"Then why did you pick a public place to have it?" I reminded her. "Oh, look. You dropped something."

I carefully juggled the picture frame and candlestick in one hand while I bent to retrieve the ring, since it was a shame to leave a five-carat princess-cut diamond ring lying on the dirty ground. Heaven only knew how many feet, hooves, and paws had trampled over the same dirt.

"Thank you," Violet said, as I handed her the ring. "It belonged to Foster's great-great-grandmother."

"I know. He told us." I turned to leave, since I'd accomplished my goal for the moment.

If the two women couldn't even be civil to each other, I'd rather play referee now than see the argument escalate.

"He didn't even tell us he was going to give it away," Violet said.

"He didn't have to," Lorelei countered. "The ring belonged to him, fair and square. But since you want it so badly, you can keep it."

I shook my head as I strolled away from their argument. They didn't even pretend to like each other. There was some bad blood between those two, and it was anyone's guess why.

I continued to walk until I reached the pull-through drive-in. That was where I spied Lance, who stood by one of the water towers. "Hey, Lance!"

He shaded his eyes from the sun as he looked for me on the horizon. I moved over to his side, my footfalls creating the only sound within earshot.

"Hi...I looked for you by the wine cellar, but you'd already left." A trickle of sweat worked its way down my cheek and stopped just shy of my chin. "You'll never believe the conversation I just overheard."

He eyed the booty in my hand curiously before he focused on the crux of my comment. "Really? Tell me about it."

"I happened to find Violet and Lorelei having a private conversation." I rolled my eyes, since I couldn't understand why they'd fight in plain view of the main house. "Anyway, Violet asked for the engagement ring back."

Lance grunted. "Huh. Now, I'm no expert, but I thought the ring always stays with the girl, even if the wedding doesn't happen."

"You're right. Though how you know that is anyone's guess."

"I read the newspaper. And Dear Abby always says the girl doesn't have to return it. By the way, what's that in your hands?"

"These are the things I got from Buck Liddell. He was trying to leave the property with them." I held out the candlestick and jeweled photo frame, which I'd managed to balance in one arm.

Lance's eyes widened. "Did those come from here?"

"Sure enough. Buck tried to hide them in a suitcase. He said Mrs. Honeycutt wants him to appraise them at his dad's antiques store. But I don't know…"

"I'm glad you took those away. For all we know, he was trying to make a getaway and thought those things would come in handy if he needed cash."

"That's what I thought. Here…I'd feel better if you took them." I carefully placed the candlestick and frame in his hands.

"Fair enough. I'll take these back to the squad car. Why don't you go look for Mrs. Honeycutt, and we'll get her side of the story."

"Gotcha. She's probably near her daughter's room. That is, unless Stormie had other plans for her."

Lance shot me a funny look. "You really don't like that newscaster, do you?"

It was hard to tell whether he was curious or simply amused by my relationship with Stormie.

"It's not that I dislike her so much. Well, maybe a little. But I don't trust her. Stormie's the type who will say or do anything to make herself look better."

"Why do you let her get under your skin like that? If you know what she's like, you should just accept it and move on."

"It's not that easy. For some reason, we keep running into each other. I think she's trying to shadow me or something."

"Well, you know what they say about small towns." Lance chuckled, which meant he really did think our relationship was funny. "Even if you don't know what you're doing at any given moment, someone else will."

"Very funny, Lance. I'll remember that the next time she and I cross paths."

I turned to leave, anxious now to escape the noon heat and slip into the air-conditioned hallways of the main house.

Thoughts of the argument between Violet and Lorelei stayed with me, though, as I scurried down the walk. Not to mention the items in Buck's suitcase. If Nelle wanted Buck to appraise those things so badly, why didn't she just ship them to his father's store in New Orleans? Or, better yet, have Buck appraise the objects right here, since this was where they belonged?

I debated those options as I crossed the property, prepared to finally find Nelle. I'd almost made it to the staircase when my cell buzzed again.

"Oh, shine." I quickly withdrew the phone. At this rate, I was never going to find out whether Buck Liddell was lying or not. "Hello?"

"Missy?"

I immediately relaxed. My favorite assistant—who also happened to be maid of honor at my wedding—always managed to cheer me up.

"Hi, Beatrice!"

"How's everything going over there?"

Of course, she knew all about Wesley Carmichael by now. People couldn't wait to share bad news in our town…but only if it happened to someone else.

"It's been a rough morning. Lorelei is devastated, of course. And the medical examiner found an extra pair of footprints by the body, so she's treating it as a homicide. But please don't tell anyone that. I don't want anyone to panic about a murderer being loose."

"No, you're right. I won't breathe a word. Do you need any help down there?"

I paused to think it over, since Beatrice was a pro at handling details I couldn't get to. It happened all the time at our store, when she rode herd over the thousand and one things that needed to be done while I was tied up with a client, vendor, or another shopkeeper.

"I can't think of anything at the moment, but I'll let you know if I think of something. How are things going at the studio?"

She didn't answer for a beat or two.

"Beatrice?"

"Nothing's going on over here. Same old, same old. You know…just another crazy Saturday morning during the wedding season. Ha, ha." Her laughter sounded hollow, though. "Nothing you haven't seen a million times before."

"Beatrice Rushing, something's up. I can tell it by your voice. Out with it."

"But you've got so much other stuff going on."

Whether she knew it or not, I could read her like a book, and I didn't like the story in this one. "And?"

"And I only wanted to help you out. Really, that's all."

"Help with what?" I sounded about as suspicious as I felt. There was something she wasn't telling me, and my patience was wearing out.

"You know your veil? How you used that pretty French lace to edge the sides?"

"Yes. I love that lace."

Being a milliner, I could get any lace I wanted, including antique, impossible-to-find French lace like Alençon. That was my choice when it came to my veil, and I found a sample from the eighteen hundreds. The seller wanted five hundred dollars a yard for it, but she was willing to give me a fifty-percent discount, since I worked in the trade. Praise the Lord for my wholesaler's license, since I could never afford the lace otherwise.

"I love that lace, too," Beatrice said. "But there was a crimp on the end of it, so I thought I'd steam it out for you."

"Well, that was nice of you. But you had me worried. I thought for sure something was wrong. Don't scare me like that!"

When she didn't laugh along with me, I quickly sobered up. "Wait a minute. Did something happen to the lace?"

She didn't say anything for a moment. Finally, a little sniffle sounded over the receiver.

"Beatrice...are you crying?"

"I'm so sorry! I only wanted to get the wrinkle out!"

"But you steam veils all the time. What happened this time?"

More sniffling. "I may have gotten rust on it from the hanger."

It took a moment for me to realize what she was saying. After the morning's misadventures, I felt like throwing my cell in the nearest bayou and crawling back into bed. But that wouldn't do anyone a lick of good, so I marshalled my best attitude and tried to get my emotions in check. "First of all, here's what you shouldn't do. You shouldn't feel guilty about it. You didn't mean to stain the lace. And I'm not mad at you."

"Okay." Beatrice's voice was weak but hopeful.

"The next thing I want you to do is go to the break room and pull a lemon from the minifridge."

"A what?"

"You heard me. Go grab a lemon. Then take it back to the counter and squeeze some of the juice into one of those bowls we use for cereal."

"Are you sure?" I could almost hear her mind spinning.

"Positive. Then take the ruined spot and soak it in the juice. Don't touch it for at least an hour after that. Then rinse the lace in cold water and—tada!—the stain will be gone."

"Just like that?" Once again, she sounded cautiously hopeful.

"Yep, just like that. It's how they used to clean lace a long time ago. Oh, and one more thing."

"Anything. What?"

"You might want to check around the studio and see if someone left behind a doll that looks like me. A doll with pins sticking out of it."

She began to chuckle, but she stopped when I didn't join in. "Wait a minute. You're not serious, are you?"

"Somewhat. This is the worst string of luck I've had in a long time."

Although I didn't believe in voodoo spells or potions, I'd learned a thing or two about them since I moved to Bleu Bayou three years ago. People on the bayou sometimes created effigies of people they didn't like. Then they stuck different colored pins in the dolls, depending on what they were trying to do. If they wanted to help someone, they might use blue pins, which stood for love, or red, which stood for power. In my case, the person must've chosen black pins, because those were guaranteed to cause something bad to happen.

"You don't believe in all that stuff, do you?" Beatrice asked.

"Not really. But guess what? You're the third person to call me today with bad news. First came one of the d'Aulnay sisters. She told me there was a fire on the *Riverboat Queen* last night, and now we can't use it for our venue. Not only that, but our photographer agreed to shoot someone else's wedding on the same day as ours. The very same day! Everything's falling apart, Beatrice, and there's nothing I can do about it."

"Hmmm." Once more, I could almost hear her mind whirring. "Since you don't need me down there, what if I make a few phone calls today at the studio? I could try to scare up another photographer for you, or maybe another place to have the wedding."

"That would be great. But only if you have time. I'm sure you've probably got a million other things going on down there. And, seriously, don't give another thought to the rust stain. I think it'll come out."

"Okay. To be honest, I was afraid to tell you at first, and I didn't even know about the other stuff that happened."

With that, we said goodbye, and I tucked the cell into my pocket. At this rate, it was anyone's guess what new calamity would befall me next, and the day was only half over.

Chapter 10

By the time I got back to the mansion, I could finally hear other voices echoing down the halls. Apparently, people got tired of waiting in their rooms by themselves, so they ventured outside to find some company.

I headed for the kitchen first, where I thought I might find Nelle. A few people milled around the counter, but Nelle wasn't one of them. *What about the sunroom?* Since I hadn't visited that room recently, what with the telephone calls and all, I decided to head there next.

I made it past the foyer, but I stopped in the hall when I spotted Lance leaning against the wall. He had his cell to his ear and was frowning.

He gestured when he noticed me, which meant I should wait for him to finish. He hung up from the call a second later and then returned the cell to his pocket. "Hey there."

"Hey, yourself. I tried to find Nelle for you, but she's nowhere to be found."

"Don't worry about that now. I just got an interesting phone call from headquarters."

"Really? Was it about Wesley's murder?"

He shook his head. "No, something else. It's about the arson investigator out of Baton Rouge."

"Baton Rouge? What about the fire department here in St. James Parish?"

"Well, the team up north has access to more lab equipment. Anyway, remember that old paddle-wheeler called the *Riverboat Queen*? The one docked on the edge of the Mississippi?"

My eyes widened. "Remember it? I was going to have my wedding there."

"Then I guess you already know about the blaze. The insurance investigator went out there this morning and found something suspicious in the kitchen."

That sparked a memory. While I didn't know Brandy d'Aulnay before this, I could almost hear her voice as she explained how the fire started.

"I heard the kitchen was gutted. Brandy d'Aulnay—she's one of the owner's daughters—called me early this morning and told me it was an electrical fire. She also said something about her dad renovating the ship, and they thought that's what caused it."

"That's what they told their insurance agent, too. How well do you know the d'Aulnays?"

I frowned. "Not very. I made a wedding veil for Sabine d'Aulnay once, but she was about as difficult as her dad."

"Why do you say that?"

"Because she practically invented the backhanded compliment."

Lance threw me a curious look, which meant he had no idea what I was talking about. While most people offered true compliments, Sabine employed that staple of the South, the backhanded one. She seemed to have mastered the art of it, which involved lobbing thinly veiled insults at someone, only delivering the message in a sugary tone. While I'd used them a time or two, including my favorite one, "Bless your heart," Sabine elevated the practice to a high-art form. She was especially fond of saying, "Isn't that special?" and the ever-popular, "I'll pray for you."

I shook my head to dislodge her voice from it. "They don't think the d'Aulnays purposefully set the fire to the ship, do they?"

Lance nodded. "It's a possibility. The investigator found an accelerant near the scene. Motorboat fuel."

"But that could've come from anywhere. The boat was docked near several others, right?"

He smiled at me. "See? Now you're thinking like a detective. They're not just looking at the accelerant, though, but at where the fire started."

"I get it. They want to see if it really originated with the electrical system or not."

"Bingo." He chewed his lower lip for a moment. "Did the business seem to be thriving to you when you booked your wedding there?"

"Now that you mention it…no." A while ago, Christophe d'Aulnay, the patriarch of the family, complained about how few tourists seemed to be coming to the Mississippi. At first, I thought maybe he was only saying that because he wanted to purchase a dock from a local landowner and he thought the owner would sympathize with him if he claimed to be broke. Now, I wasn't so sure.

"We'll know more this afternoon," Lance said. "They're analyzing the electrical components now, and they're going to try to unravel where the fuel came from."

"I can't believe someone would purposefully set fire to a historical landmark like the *Riverboat Queen.*" I frowned, although Lance had provided some compelling evidence. Maybe I didn't *want* to believe it.

"You'd be surprised. Look at those three churches that burned. One of them was a hundred years old."

The idea of arson left a sour taste in my mouth. With its ruby-red paint and forest-green accents, the boat offered a unique look at life on the Mississippi a century ago. Why would someone try to destroy that?

"Anyway," he said, "I have enough going on with this murder right now. I have some more calls to make, so I'll catch you later."

He bid his goodbyes, and then he disappeared down the hall. Once he turned the corner, I resumed my trek to the sunroom, where the door stood open. Two people already sat on the wicker sofa, their backs to me, but neither one looked like Nelle.

Lorelei was there, since her jet-black hair and messy ponytail were hard to miss, but a gentleman sat next to her. Tufts of wispy fur peeked over the top of the gentleman's vest, so I guessed she sat with Jamie, the florist, on the sofa.

"You poor baby," he said.

Sure enough, the moment he spoke, I realized I was right.

He gently patted Lorelei's shoulder afterward.

"What am I going to do?' Her voice was soft and anguished.

I debated turning around right then and there and leaving the room, since I'd heard more than my share of private conversations that morning, but something about their posture gave me pause. They sat shoulder to shoulder, as if they were best friends or something, and not a bride and her wedding florist.

"There's nothing you can do. It's all in the hands of the police now."

"But do you think he suffered? I would just die if I thought for one moment he was in a lot of pain at the end."

This time, he gently squeezed her shoulder. "Try not to think about it. It'll only upset you more."

"You're right. I know you're right. It all feels so surreal."

"There, there." Jamie moved his hand up and lightly tipped her head onto his shoulder.

I craned my neck, hoping to gauge Lorelei's reaction, when my toe caught on the edge of a throw rug and I tumbled forward. Before I knew what was happening, I landed smack-dab on the ground. The thwack of my kneecap hitting the hard floor rang out and both of them spun around. "Missy!" Lorelei jumped up and hurried over to me. "Are you okay?" She leaned down and offered her hand, which I gratefully accepted.

"Thank you." I pulled myself upright, and then I mentally scanned my body for injuries. "I think I'm okay. I didn't mean to interrupt your conversation."

Jamie scowled at me. Unlike Lorelei, he didn't seem concerned for my welfare. "What are you doing here?"

"I was trying to find Nelle."

"She's not here," Lorelei said. "I haven't been upstairs in a while, though. I ran into Jamie here"—she flung her hand out to indicate the florist—"so I never made it back to my room. Have you tried upstairs yet?"

"Not yet." I plastered on a smile to indicate my good intentions. "Again, I'm sorry I interrupted you."

"That's okay. I should probably head upstairs anyway." Lorelei turned around to face her friend. "Bye, Jamie. Thanks for everything."

She hurried from the room, and the man's gaze trailed after her.

"I honestly didn't think I'd find anyone here," I said.

"Well, you did. I should go, too." Ice coated his voice. "Maybe next time you can announce yourself when you enter a room. That's the polite thing to do."

"You're right." Now that the shock had worn off, my knee throbbed. "Think I'll get some ice from the kitchen. These floors are really hard."

Jamie brushed past me on his way from the room. "Don't worry about the floors. They're a hundred years old. They've gone through a lot worse."

For someone who spoke so tenderly to Lorelei only a minute ago, the change in his tone was striking. I had seen two sides of the same coin, only one side said "friend" and the other said "foe." Somehow, I'd managed to land on the "foe" side, and there was no telling if that would ever change.

* * * *

The rest of the afternoon passed uneventfully. I returned to the kitchen and looked around for Nelle, but I was unsuccessful. I *did* manage to locate some ice cubes for my throbbing knee, however, along with a baggie to put them in.

The moment I applied the makeshift ice bag to the sore spot, the bridesmaid from breakfast, who let me sit at her table, entered the room. She didn't seem to notice me, though, since she studied a sheaf of papers she held.

"Hello."

"Oh, hi." She glanced up. "Can you believe all this? It's the guest list for the wedding. How am I ever going to call all these people and tell them the wedding's been cancelled?"

"Good point. By the way, I didn't introduce myself earlier. I'm Melissa DuBois, but my friends call me Missy."

"Nice to meet you."

Between the papers in her hand and the bag of ice in mine, we both nodded in lieu of shaking hands.

"I didn't catch your name," I said.

"Sheridan. Sheridan English. Only, everyone calls me Sherry."

"You've got a great last name." I tried to lighten the mood by smiling. "Say...would you like me to help you with the guest list?"

"Would I?" She sounded pleasantly surprised. "I'd love it! Do you think you could take half the list?"

"Sure." Although I wanted to find Nelle and quiz her about the antiques in Buck's suitcase, it couldn't take *that* long to call a few people, could it?

"Great! I'll give you a hundred names, and I'll take the rest. Thank you so much!" She happily divided the paperwork before she thrust half of it at me. "You don't know what a relief this is!"

I gulped as I accepted the assignment. I had no idea we were talking about that many names. I thought she'd ask me to contact maybe twenty people. Thirty, tops. Now that I'd offered, though, I couldn't exactly take it back. "Okay, then. I think I'll make my calls in the hall. See you soon."

I limped away from the kitchen, since she seemed to want to make her calls there, and I decided to make mine in the hall. After a while, I ended up sliding to the floor, since it was too hard to juggle a soggy bag of ice in one hand and a cell phone in the other.

The hours dragged by. Finally, I hung up from the last call and straightened, the pain in my knee nothing compared to the way my ear ached.

I headed for the kitchen, relieved to finally be done with the chore. "I'm finished." I hurriedly stepped into the kitchen.

Sheridan didn't seem to hear me. Instead, she still clutched the pages to her chest, only now she angled her body to avoid being interrupted. I skidded to a stop just as she said something into the telephone.

"That's right," she whispered. "It's over. The wedding's off."

At first, I didn't understand what she was talking about. Maybe because of the way she whispered, or because she sounded more relieved about the news than upset.

When I called wedding guests, I tried to break the news as gently as possible, while still giving them the pertinent details. It took a fine mix of sympathy and straightforwardness to get the job done, but I think I'd managed to walk the tightrope fairly well.

Sheridan obviously wasn't concerned about doing that. In fact, she actually giggled after a moment.

"Can you believe it?" she said into the receiver. "It's like a dream come true!"

A dream? I squinted at the back of her neck. Every other person I spoke to this weekend considered the news more a nightmare than a dream. And the chuckle was a little over the top.

I pointedly cleared my throat. "Ahem."

She flinched at the noise, and then she slowly turned around, the cell falling to her side. "Oh. Hello there."

I nodded at the phone in her hand, since she obviously forgot to say goodbye. "I think you forgot something."

"What? Oh, yeah. Right." She quickly mumbled goodbye and clicked off the call. "That was, um, my sister. That's it. It was my younger sister. She knew Wesley, too."

"Really." For some reason, the explanation didn't hold water. Maybe it was the way she wouldn't look at me or the way she conveniently "forgot" who she was talking to.

"Did you finish the names I gave you?" She had changed the subject rather awkwardly, and we both knew it.

"I did. What about you?"

"Same. Almost. I have a few more to go."

By now, she seemed to have pulled herself back together. She gestured for my notes, which I gladly handed over.

"Thanks," she said. "I've got seven more people to call, and then I'll be done, too. By the way…someone told me Mrs. Honeycutt wants us to stay for dinner tonight. Something about the caterer and how she couldn't stop the order. Everyone's eating in the dining room."

"That would be great. To be honest, I haven't eaten a thing all day." Given everything that had happened, I completely forgot about the rumble in my stomach…until now. "I'm starving."

"Like I said, she's going to serve it in the dining room. Save me a seat?"

I waffled. "Sure…I guess." It was hard for me to forget the joy in her voice when she told her "sister" about Wesley's death. What else was she hiding? "Um, good luck with the rest of the calls."

I quickly moved away, but I cast a final glance over my shoulder before I reached the hall. Like I expected, Sheridan stared at my retreating back, and she had yet to return the phone to her ear. She seemed to be waiting for me to leave.

Well, that's odd. And totally unexpected, considering how friendly the girl had been to me earlier.

I momentarily forgot about Sheridan, though, when a rumble worked its way through my empty stomach. I continued to walk toward the dining room, and, after a few feet, I heard the welcome sound of serving utensils clattering against chaffing dishes and flatware pinging the sides of dinner plates.

Unlike the kitchen, which was bright and airy, with stainless-steel appliances, recessed lights, and cool white paint, the dining room looked gloriously dark and moody. Very Victorian. Rich wood panels covered the walls, and an enormous crystal chandelier dripped clear orbs of glass.

While most dining room tables seated six or eight, this one could easily accommodate twenty-four. Maybe twenty-six if someone added extra chairs at the ends. The caterers had removed the chairs from the table, though, and pushed them up against the wall.

Shiny silver chafing dishes paraded down the table's middle, with matching utensils paired with each one.

Several people already milled around the room, including Wesley's stepsister, Electra; Daryl Tibodeaux, who still wore his coveralls; and the best man, Buck Liddell, who was dressed in a natty blue blazer and striped bowtie. Thankfully, Stormie and her cameraman either weren't invited to stay, or they weren't hungry.

"I hope you enjoy the meal," a voice whispered behind me.

I turned to see Nelle, who anxiously appraised the table, like a general inspecting his troops.

"There you are!" I said. "I've been looking for you all afternoon."

"Really?"

At that moment, the smell of seared meat and garlic potatoes wafted over to me. "Thank you for inviting us to dinner."

"It was the least I could do, dear. I couldn't very well send everyone back home on an empty stomach, now could I?"

"Speaking of which…" I leaned closer, since I didn't want to broadcast our conversation to the room, "have you spoken to Detective LaPorte lately? Do you know if he's going to let everyone go home tonight?"

Since I was stuck on my cell most of the afternoon, I had no idea what Lance planned to do with everyone.

"He and I finally talked a little while ago. He wants us to gather in the sunroom after dinner so he can make an announcement. I think most people will be eager to go home, though. Don't you?"

"Probably." Her mention of people going home reminded me of the reason I wanted to find her earlier. "I ran into Buck Liddell this afternoon. He told me he was going back to New Orleans. And he had several of your things with him."

"Yes, I heard about that. He told me you thought he took those things without my permission."

"In my defense, the story sounded pretty implausible." I glanced at Buck, who hovered over one of the chafing dishes at the far end of the table. He seemed to have gotten over our little row because he winked at me when he noticed me watching him.

"It was all a big misunderstanding," she said.

"So, you did tell him it was okay to bring those things to New Orleans?"

She nodded. "I did, but please don't tell my husband. I was hoping to use the money to pay for Wesley's funeral."

"Really?" I squinted. Why would Nelle want to pay for Wesley's funeral, when his parents looked perfectly capable of doing it?

"Excuse me."

We both turned to see a man hovering behind us.

He wore a stiff dinner jacket and a plastic name tag that identified him as part of the catering company. "Sorry to interrupt, but I have some questions about dessert. Would you like us to serve the wedding cake, or did you have something else in mind?"

"Dear me, I hadn't really thought about it. Maybe I should go with you to the kitchen." Nelle glanced at me sheepishly. "Will you excuse me?"

"Of course." No need for me to keep her to myself when other people needed her, too. "We can talk later. And thanks for letting me know about the antiques. I'll tell Detective LaPorte about that."

"Thank you, dear. And please don't be shy about helping yourself to the buffet. You'll find plates on the sideboard."

She walked away, my unanswered questions trailing after her. Why would she sell her family heirlooms to pay for Wesley's funeral, when that normally fell to the victim's family? Although I didn't know the Carmichaels personally, I'd heard his father was an attorney. Not to mention, Wesley attended a very expensive, private university, according to Lorelei.

The subject came up when we discussed wedding cakes, and Lorelei mentioned Wesley wanted a groom's cake topped with the logo for Southern Methodist University, which was his alma mater. Around here people called that school "Southern Millionaires University" because tuition topped out at sixty thousand a year.

And yet, Nelle felt compelled to pay for Wesley's funeral costs, in lieu of his family picking up the tab. Not only that, but why didn't she want her husband to know about it?

I mulled those questions as I gathered a plate and silverware from a heavy antique sideboard placed next to the wall. As I made my way to the table, I spied Buck, who still stood at the head of it, debating whether to add a second serving of roast beef to his already full plate. Just then, the door to the dining room burst open.

Two strange men hustled into the space. They both wore dark sunglasses, even at night, and their suits looked expensive. They must've weighed about three hundred pounds apiece, all of it muscle, judging by the way their shoulders strained against the seams of their jackets.

Conversation immediately stopped. It wasn't every day two huge men muscled their way into a room, side by side. By the time anyone realized what was happening, one of the men strode to the head of the table and grabbed Buck by the elbow.

Buck was so surprised, he tipped his plate sideways, and roast beef splattered to the floor.

We were all too shocked to move. By the time I pulled out my cell, ready to call Lance, the men had whisked Buck away from the room and into the hall.

Everything ended as quickly as it'd begun. As soon as the men disappeared, the room burst into a symphony of whispers.

"What was that?" someone gasped.

"Did anyone recognize those people?" someone else asked.

"My goodness!" An older woman with upswept hair slapped the arm of her elderly husband, who stood beside her. "Don't just stand there, Albert. Do something!"

I quickly punched the number for Lance into my cell and waited for him to pick up the call. Luckily, he answered after two rings.

"Hi, Missy."

"Lance…two men just kidnapped the best man!"

"Whoa. Slow down. Where are you?"

"The dining room. It happened a minute ago. Two thugs muscled Buck out of here before anyone could stop them."

"Okay, I'm on it. Don't move. I don't want anyone else going after those guys. You got that?"

"Got it. I'll tell everyone."

I clicked off the call and lowered my cell. By now, the room buzzed with conversation, like a swarm of bees set free of its hive.

"May I have everyone's attention, please?"

No one paid me a bit of mind, so, I cleared my throat and tried again.

"Everyone, listen! Detective LaPorte knows about what just happened. He's looking for the guys. He told us to stay here, out of harm's way."

"But—" Darryl looked unhappy with my announcement. He'd already pulled a wrench from the pocket of his coveralls, and he looked ready to use it.

"Darryl, please put that away. Let the police handle this. Those guys could have guns."

He glumly shoved the tool back where it belonged, and the buzz of conversation started all over again.

"Well, that was something!"

I turned to see Electra Carmichael, Wesley's stepsister, who had moved to my side of the room. Tonight, she wore a bright sundress, and she'd piled her red hair on top of her head. She looked like Carmen Miranda, but without the grapes or bananas.

"I agree. I only hope Lance can catch those guys before they leave the property."

"Why do you think they did that?"

"I have no idea, and I don't think anyone else does, either."

"It definitely shook up our hostess." Electra pointed at Nelle, who slumped against the wall by the exit. She looked paler than a bedsheet, and she appeared too stunned to speak.

"I'd better go make sure she's all right. Will you excuse me?"

"Sure." Electra glanced at the empty plate in my hand. "But don't forget to eat something, too. It'd be a shame to let all that expensive beef go to waste. I'm sure my stepbrother would've helped himself if he was here."

Her comment stopped me in my tracks. Judging by the conversation I'd overheard yesterday, Wesley didn't eat meat. And apparently, his stepsister didn't know that. Strange.

"I can't believe he's gone," she said. "Gone like the wind. Guess I'll never have the chance to get to know him better now."

"I suppose." I glanced furtively at Nelle, who still seemed shell-shocked. "If you don't mind—"

"It's a tragedy, that's what it is." Apparently, Electra wasn't finished with her soliloquy, and she wanted me to stay for it. "Two siblings, separated by a great distance, but longing to reconnect across the miles. Cut down by the Fates before that could happen."

"Yes, well—"

"You know what's worst of all? My stepbrother died before I could tell him the good news." She shook her head forlornly. "I only heard about it a few days ago myself, when Mother called. She can be a little, uh, controlling, you know. She never breathed a word of the trust fund until now."

Trust fund? By this time, several people had gathered around Nelle, so I felt better about staying with Electra. Especially since her words piqued my curiosity.

"You have a trust fund?" I asked.

"Yes. Mother told me there's a trust fund that comes from my stepdad's side of the family. He included me on it when he legally adopted me. That was after he and my mom got married, you know. Only Wesley and I have access to it, which I'm sure didn't make my mother happy."

"And you never told him about it?"

"I didn't have time." She hung her head again. "Not that it would've changed anything. But it would've been nice for him to find out about the money."

"I suppose."

"Not that I was curious about the amount, of course."

"Of course."

"But get this." She leaned in, and the pungent smell of wine hit me full force. I hadn't noticed she held a wineglass, which was already two-thirds empty. "She told me it's more than twenty million bucks. Twenty million bucks! Do you know how many zeros that is? Seven! I counted them on the plane ride over here."

"That's a lot of zeros." My thoughts immediately flew to Lance's police investigation. Did the police know about this? Whoever killed Wesley must've had a good reason for wanting him dead. In Electra's case, it might be closer to twenty million reasons.

"But I've said too much." Electra threw back her head and drained the last sip of wine from her glass. "Listen to me, going on and on. I'm sure you have better things to do than hear me babble about some silly little trust fund."

82   *Sandra Bretting*

"Oh, no. It's very interesting." Which was an understatement. And Lance would be just as interested to learn about it as I was. I'd have to find him on the double and fill him in on the latest turn of events. "Um, I think I should get going, though. I have, uh, some important business to discuss with one of the guests."

Luckily, Electra didn't seem offended. If anything, she seemed more concerned about finding the minibar than about losing me as her audience. "Of course. I have to find the bar, anyway. You'd think they'd bring the bottles out here so we wouldn't have to hunt for them." She stepped away, her footsteps wobbly, thanks to the wine and the sky-high stilettos she wore.

Once she disappeared, I turned to leave as well. I first passed the people comforting Nelle, and then I made my way into the hall. Between the two mysterious men and the way they muscled Buck out of the room, everyone was too busy gossiping to notice my departure.

I hurried along the corridor and made a beeline for the front door. Just as I was about to step outside, Lance walked into the foyer.

"Hey, there!" he said.

"Thank goodness you're here! Did you catch those guys?"

He looked winded, and sweat lined his brow. "Yep...just as they were about to drive away. They shoved Buck into the trunk of the car, and then they tried to act like nothing was wrong when they saw me. Turns out they work for a bookie out of Baton Rouge."

"So, Buck was involved in gambling, too?"

"We don't know that yet. They're questioning him down at the police station. My backup happened to be in the area, so she took the men down to the station for me."

"Including the two thugs?"

"Yep. They both have open warrants, so they're definitely going to jail tonight. I'm going to head back to the station after I wrap things up here."

"Speaking of which—" I glanced over my shoulder, but the hall was empty. "Nelle said you wanted to meet with everyone. Do you have any news?"

Lance quickly nodded. "I do. Let's move outside. I want you to be the first to hear it."

"Of course." I gladly followed him outside.

Once upon a time, before we became partners in crime, so to speak, Lance hoarded whatever information he got. He doled out a few snippets to me, but they would be few and far between. Now, however, he treated me like an equal when it came to solving crimes.

Everything changed when I helped him nab a murderer at Morningside Plantation. Ever since that investigation, he allowed me to read medical examiners' reports, tox records, you name it. All in exchange for my observations about the cases.

"I got a preliminary report back." Lance withdrew a slim folder from his back pocket. The cover was dark—about as dark as the inky night sky—which made it hard to read anything. I did manage to make out the seal for the St. James Parish Medical Examiner's Office, though, because it twinkled in the air, like a shiny quarter.

"What does it say?" Sometimes Lance summarized reports for me, which made it easier for both of us.

"Basically, the ME found traces of an herb called thorn apple in the lining of the victim's lungs."

I cocked my head. "Thorn apple? I've never heard of that before."

While I had become acquainted with some of the herbs that grew on the bayou, thanks to another killer who made use of a little-known plant called jack-in-the-pulpit, I'd never once heard of thorn apple.

"Its real name is Datura, and some folks call it jimson weed. It's very toxic when the plant is young. It only takes about ten milligrams to kill someone."

"But how would someone give it to him without him knowing it?"

"It's not that hard, when you think about it. People crush up the seeds, and then they either ingest it, or they smoke it. It's a hallucinogenic."

"Smoke it? You don't mean…"

"Bingo. Forensics found traces of the same herb on the cigarette paper we found in the wine cellar."

"So someone gave the cigarette to Wesley, but first they doctored it with thorn apple. That's really ingenious. Not to mention diabolical."

"Right." Lance opened the report to the first page, which listed all of Wesley's biographical information. "He weighed about one seventy, so he probably felt the effects within an hour."

"What does thorn apple do?"

"Everything…it causes nausea, vomiting, hallucinations. It makes people delirious."

"But that doesn't sound lethal."

"No, it doesn't." Lance returned the report to his pocket. "But it can cause a chain reaction in the body. First comes respiratory distress and then tachycardia. He probably died from a heart attack."

"Okay, so it sounds like you know *how* he died. But you still don't know *who* killed him, or *why*."

"True, but that's what I'm hoping to find out tonight. And a good place to start is with the people in there." He pointed to the house, which glowed like an enormous hurricane lamp in the dark.

"Are you going to tell everyone what's in the medical examiner's report?"

"Maybe. Or maybe not. Maybe I'll let one of them tell me what happened."

"Well, now. That would be interesting."

He threw me a sly smile. "Wouldn't it? I have a feeling someone in there could tell us the whole story: beginning, middle, and end."

Chapter 11

We both turned, but before either of us could move toward the house, I remembered something else.

"Wait a minute, Lance. I had an interesting conversation with Electra Carmichael a little while ago. She's Wesley's stepsister."

"I know. She's an actress out of New York City."

"Well, she told me she's coming into a ton of money from a trust fund."

"A trust fund?" Lance cocked his head. "How much money are we talking about?"

"Twenty million dollars. She was supposed to get half. It's coming from her stepdad's side of the family."

Now he squinted as well. "Don't trust funds usually benefit blood relatives?"

"Usually. But she said her stepdad legally adopted her when he married Electra's mom. Wesley was supposed to get half, and Electra would get the other half. But that was before Wesley died."

"Did he even know about the money?" Lance asked.

"No, he didn't. That's the interesting part. Electra's mother only told her about it last week. And Wesley had no idea he stood to inherit so much."

"Hmmm." Lance's squint remained. "That means Electra had a good reason for wanting her stepbrother out of the picture. Even though he was family."

"Here's the thing." I moved closer to Lance, although we were the only two people outside. "They weren't a very close family. She didn't know anything about his life. Not that he couldn't practice law or that he'd become a vegetarian, even."

"Well, listen to you."

"What?"

"You're starting to sound like a bona fide detective, Miss DuBois. Maybe I should be concerned for my job now."

"Very funny. But seriously. Here Electra was going to inherit all this money, and now her stepbrother's dead. Not only that, but Nelle told me she wanted to sell some of her family's treasures to pay for Wesley's funeral."

"His funeral?" Lance still looked confused, as if the tidbits were coming too fast to process. "Really? But Wesley's father is a big-time corporate attorney up in Baton Rouge. Why wouldn't he pay for the funeral?"

"I don't know. It's not something people usually do if the victim's family can afford to handle it. I don't understand it either."

"Looks like we're going to have an interesting chat tonight," he said.

With that, we both returned our attention to the mansion. Everything looked so calm on the outside. A neat row of hedges passed under the staircase, and the two water towers provided perfect bookends, one on either side.

No one driving past would ever suspect such a pretty building held such dark secrets.

* * * *

By the time Lance and I arrived in the sunroom, most of the bridal party was already there. Several bridesmaids perched wearily on the wicker furniture, their chins propped on their palms, while the groomsmen either leaned against a wall or sat on the floor. Even Darryl was there, although by now he'd changed out of his coveralls and into a clean work shirt and jeans.

No one spoke. Whereas before, people tried to chat about this, that, or the other thing, now they didn't even try. It was as if everyone wanted to get off the property as soon as possible and forget this day ever happened.

Lorelei sat on the sofa again, next to Jamie. Even Violet Carmichael was there, her back ramrod straight as she sat next to her husband.

Lance walked into the room ahead of me, and everyone's gaze turned to him when he made his way to the front. "Thank you all for coming tonight. I know it's been a long day. I'm sure everyone wants to get out of here."

"Tell that to Buck." It was one of the groomsmen, and he spoke just loudly enough for everyone to hear. "That guy didn't have a choice about whether to leave or not."

"I heard that," Lance said. "I'm sure you all know by now we took the men who kidnapped Buck Liddell into custody. They both had outstanding warrants, so they'll be spending the night in jail."

"But who *were* they?" It was Sheridan, and she sounded baffled.

"They were hired by some bookie in Baton Rouge. We know the guy. He runs an illegal gambling operation at Evangeline Downs Race Track."

Foster Carmichael stirred. "Did you say Evangeline Downs?"

"Yes." Lance turned his way. "The guy's the head of a large bookmaking operation. They bet on horses down there. Why...do you know the place?"

Before Foster could speak, his wife clamped her hand on his knee.

"No, of course not. He doesn't know anything about a racetrack," she said. "Don't pay any attention to Foster. He's very confused right now."

"Is that true, Mr. Carmichael?" Lance asked. "Or do you have some information that could help us out?"

With great effort, Foster swatted his wife's hand away. "Yes, I've heard of the racetrack. Everyone in Louisiana knows about it."

"But did your son go there a lot?" Lance asked.

"I'm afraid so. It's no secret Wesley had a gambling problem. He and his friend Buck both did."

"And they talked about that specific racetrack?"

Violet moved to speak, but she took one look at Lance's face and must have thought the better of it. Which encouraged her husband to finally speak his mind. "Wesley did talk about it a time or two. But he called it a casino. He said something about going there to try and win his money back."

"The racetrack also has a full casino," Lance agreed. "With slots and tables. But could your son have been in debt to the racetrack bookie, too?"

"Anything's possible. I think both my son and his friend got themselves into trouble over there."

"Well, that's just one part of our investigation." Lance returned his attention to the room at large now. "We also got a preliminary toxicology report back from the lab today. We know what killed Wesley Carmichael."

An electric shock passed through the room.

"The medical examiner found a toxic herb in the lining of his lungs. Something called thorn apple."

Everyone looked so confused.

Lance immediately spoke again. "It's also called jimson weed or moon flower. The technical name is *Datura stramonium*. Basically, it's a hallucinogen that can be fatal if given at a high-enough dose."

"Didja say jimson weed?" Darryl perched on a stool at the side of the room. He'd found the stool by the globe that opened up to a bar, and he sat half-on, half-off the stool's cushion. "We gots lotsa dat plant 'round here. Flowers in da summertime, right 'bout now."

"Yes, it does." Lance nodded. "People used to apply it as an analgesic in the old days, and some people still use it to treat asthma."

"Asthma?" Now it was Lorelei's turn to speak up. She'd been leaning her head on Jamie's shoulder, but she quickly straightened. "You don't say. Everyone knows my fiancé had asthma. He was angry with himself because he forgot to bring his inhaler this weekend."

"Well, we also found traces of the plant on some evidence that was left behind," Lance continued. "Someone rolled the leaves into a cigarette paper that was left on the floor. It was a rookie mistake, because whoever did it should've been more careful to remove the evidence."

The silence remained, as thick as smoke. Either people had no idea what Lance was talking about, or they didn't want to admit it.

"But my son didn't smoke," Foster finally said. "He thought it was a nasty habit."

"Did he, now?" Lance said. "Well, that's what we're dealing with. Since we don't have enough leads to go on at this point, I'm going to ask everyone to stay close by if they can. I'll pick up the investigation in the morning."

"That's asking a lot of us, Detective." Finally, Violet found her voice too. "I don't intend to spend the night where my son died."

"Obviously, I can't make you stay here," Lance said. "But I'd like to interview you all again tomorrow morning. One of you might remember something that could break this case wide open."

"Well, that's...that's just...not going to happen." Violet stumbled over her words. "And I can't believe you even suggested it."

"I'm sorry, Mrs. Carmichael." Lance shrugged. "But if it's too traumatic for you, I understand."

"I don't mind." It was Foster, and he spoke quietly. "If you think it will help, I'll stay here as long as it takes."

"Thank you. And you, Mrs. Carmichael? Are you willing to join your husband and stay here tonight?"

"All right. I guess I can stay, too. But I'd like a room as far away from the water tower as possible. The one where you found Wesley's body."

"Of course, dear." Nelle rose from her chair in the middle of the room. "I wouldn't think of giving you a bedroom anywhere near where your son died. Please use the master bedroom. It's at the back of the house, so it's very private."

"You're too kind." Violet and Nelle locked eyes, and something unspoken passed between the two women. "You're always so kind."

"Anyone can stay," Nelle said. "We're very fortunate to have ten bedrooms, so there's plenty of space if some of us don't mind sharing."

"Thank you, Mrs. Honeycutt." Lance glanced at his watch. "Look, it's almost eight now. Let's call it a night and convene here tomorrow morning at seven. I'll start my interviews shortly after that. Good night."

People began to stir, and sound softly rippled through the room. After a moment, though, another sound joined it, which was mechanical and harsh, compared to the crowd's quiet stirring.

It was a car, which stalled by the front door, and, after a moment, the harsh squeak of metal rubbing against metal sounded as someone opened and closed the car door.

A few seconds later, Buck appeared on the landing to the sunroom, his face ashen.

"Buck!" Lorelei was the first to notice him, and she dashed to the door as soon as he arrived. "We were so worried about you!" She threw her arms around his neck and gave him a quick hug. "Whatever happened?"

He didn't answer, but the ghostly cast of his face spoke volumes.

Chapter 12

The best man glanced around the room quickly, but his gaze flitted from one spot to the next, as if he couldn't quite focus.

"Buck?" Lorelei's voice wavered. "Are you okay?"

Slowly, but surely, he extracted himself from her embrace, and then he headed for the minibar at the back of the room. He haphazardly threw the lid open and plucked out a whiskey bottle.

"Is everything okay, son?" Lance called out.

"I.,.I think so."

While Buck poured a drink, I dodged around people in order to reach him. He tipped back his head and gulped the whiskey just as Lorelei arrived, too.

"Ah," he said. "I'm much better now."

"What happened?" I asked. "What did those men want?"

"They wanted me." He sounded awestruck. "That's what they wanted. Me."

"We all guessed that." Lance joined us at the back of the room.

No one seemed to notice our conversation, because everyone else was too busy making plans for the night.

Once I stood next to Buck, I saw the rough scratches all over his face. They extended to his neck, where they crisscrossed the skin between his chin and collarbone.

"It looks like they roughed you up," I said.

"They started to." He chuckled, but it was bitter. "But then they threw me in the trunk of the car when Detective LaPorte here came along."

When he gestured at Lance, I noticed his antique cuff link was gone. Wispy threads trailed from the buttonhole to his wrist, where the link used to lie.

"Oh, no!" I said. "They stole your antique cuff links."

"They did. But the police got 'em back at the station. They tried to take my wallet, my car keys, you name it. I'm surprised they didn't turn me upside down and shake everything out of my pockets."

"Let me guess…they wanted to settle your gambling debts." Leave it to Lance to get right to the heart of the matter.

"But I didn't owe them anything," Buck insisted. "It was all Wesley's fault. I paid them back last year. It took me a ton of overtime at my dad's business, but I somehow managed."

"So why'd they rough you up?" I didn't understand why a bookie would go after Buck if he'd already paid his debt.

"Because they can't get anything from Wesley now." The bitterness was back. "My best friend left this world owing his bookie one hundred thousand dollars."

Lorelei gasped, and we all turned to face her. She looked caught between doubt and horror, and it was anyone's guess which side would win.

"Are you sure?' she whispered. "That's a lot of money."

"Tell me about it. I thought for sure I was a goner."

I debated whether to whisk Lorelei away from our conversation right then and there. No need to talk about Wesley's bad choices in front of her, when she'd already suffered enough. "Would you like me to help you up to your room?"

She seemed so fragile now, and even paler than before.

"No." She shook her head resolutely. "I need to hear everything that happened with Wesley. I don't want anyone to coddle me. Please. I'm going to find out anyway."

"Okay, then." If the girl didn't want my help, I couldn't exactly force it on her.

"Anyway," Buck said, "those guys came here tonight to collect on Wesley's tab. But then they found out about the water tower." He cut his gaze to Lorelei. "I'm sorry, but I really thought they were gonna kill me when they couldn't get to Wesley."

"Or maybe something else happened." I turned to Lance the moment I thought of it. "Do you think maybe they were the ones who killed him?'

"Not really," Lance said. "That bookie isn't known for wiping people out. He's known for extortion, and definitely blackmail. But not murder."

I mentally flipped through the various scenarios. If Buck was right, and the men meant to hurt—or even kill—him, they didn't do a very good job of it. To me, it seemed like they were more focused on robbing him. But Wesley was another story. What if they found out he couldn't pay them back?

"I don't know, Lance," I said. "Maybe they came here last night and lured Wesley to the wine cellar."

"But that's not how this bookie operates." Lance didn't waver. "We have his thugs in custody, though, so we'll know more after the interrogation."

Buck still didn't look convinced, and he sloppily poured himself another whiskey. "It sure felt like they were gonna kill me." He threw his head back and downed the second drink as fast as he could. "I saw my life flash before my eyes."

"You poor thing," Lorelei softly said. "I don't think you ought to drive anywhere tonight. You've had too much of a shock."

And too much to drink, I wanted to add, although I bit my tongue.

"Mom's putting people up in our house tonight," she continued. "Please stay."

"I doubt if she wants me here. Me and Wesley have been nothing but trouble."

"That's not true." Lorelei shook her head. "You tried to do the right thing by paying that bookie back. I'm just sorry Wesley didn't do the same thing. Please stay."

"Well..." Little by little, Buck's face relaxed. Either he knew she was right, or the alcohol was starting to take effect. "Okay. I guess so. Thanks, Lorelei."

He set the empty glass on a side table and turned to leave. When he made his way across the room to join Nelle, a new voice spoke up.

"May I speak with you a moment, detective?"

We all turned to see Violet Carmichael, who had stepped up behind us.

"Of course," Lance said. "How can I help you?"

"I'd prefer to speak to you *alone*." Her tone, not to mention a look she threw Lorelei and me, was pointed. "Please. It's important."

"That's okay." By now, Lorelei was too exhausted to put up a fight. "I was just leaving. My head really hurts, and I want to go to bed."

As soon as she scooted around Violet, the older woman flinched.

"Now, what's on your mind?" Lance asked.

"Completely alone." Violet said.

"No...Missy can stay. Whatever you have to say to me, you can say in front of Miss DuBois."

"Very well." His refusal took some of the wind out of her sails, but it didn't stop her altogether. "I wanted to tell you about something I overhead yesterday. It might be important."

"By all means…tell me what you know." Lance slowly withdrew a notepad from the pocket of his khakis. It was the same notepad I'd seen him use countless times during countless interviews.

"Well, I was walking through the garden yesterday, and I heard my son talking with *that* girl."

That girl? Interesting how much Violet disliked Lorelei.

"What were they talking about?" Lance asked.

"They were fighting. I could hear them, clear as day. It happened right around six last evening."

"And you're sure of the time?" Lance scribbled something or other onto his notepad. But all the while, his gaze remained locked on Violet.

"Definitely six," she said. "I'd bet my life on it. They were arguing about the ceremony. I don't think Wesley wanted to go through with it. And I think maybe Lorelei knows more about my son's killing than she's letting on."

"How dare you!"

For the second time that night, someone new barged into our conversation. Now it was Jamie, who glowered behind Violet. Jamie brought with him the scent of Paco Rabanne, which he'd applied a little too liberally. "You have no right to say that! None at all."

"But…but—"

"Officer, don't pay any attention to her," Jamie continued. "She's trying to cover up for that no-good son of hers. Wesley was trouble from day one. Trouble! He didn't deserve a woman like Lorelei. His mother should be ashamed of herself."

"Why, I never!" Finally, Violet found her voice. "You have no right to speak to me that way!"

All around us, people stopped chatting when they noticed a fight was brewing in our corner of the room.

"It's a wonder Lorelei didn't call off the wedding," Jamie said. "Your son was no choir boy, you know."

"Okay, you two." Lance moved to separate them. "Let's keep it civil."

"But it's true, officer," Jamie said. "She's trying to shift the blame for what happened to Lorelei. And that's the last person she should be pointing her finger at."

"You don't know what you're talking about," Violet fired back. "I'm just telling the detective what I heard. And how dare you speak to me like that!"

"Look, fighting isn't going to help anyone." I scrambled to diffuse the tension. "And people are starting to stare."

Sure enough, that did the trick, and they both fell silent. I should've appealed to their vanity from the start.

"That's better," Lance said.

"In fact, I'll help you find Nelle." I placed my hand on Violet's wrist, which was trembling. "We can see about getting you settled into that master bedroom."

The way I figured it, Violet had already told Lance what she knew. Now he'd want to interview Jamie, who seemed to have his own reason for hijacking the conversation.

Lance nodded. "That's a good idea, Missy. I have a few questions for Mr. Lee here."

"You're welcome." I started to lead Violet away, but we didn't get very far.

"Never mind," Jamie said. "I don't have anything more to say. I just wanted everyone to know Lorelei had nothing to do with this whole mess. Nothing! If anything, she's a victim here, too." With that, he turned and hurried away, as quickly as he'd appeared.

I expected Lance to follow him, but he didn't. He did, however, check something in his notes as he flipped the pad closed.

"Do you have any idea what he was talking about, Mrs. Carmichael?" he asked.

"No. None at all." Interestingly enough, she gazed over Lance's right shoulder this time. "I have no idea what he was talking about. What a strange little man. But if you'll excuse me, I think I'd better find the master bedroom. I'm terribly tired, you know."

The moment she left, I swallowed hard. For some reason, the confrontation between Violet and Jamie left a strange taste in my mouth. It was anyone's guess who was telling the truth and who wasn't.

Chapter 13

Lance and I watched her walk away, the last of the guests to leave the sunroom.

"Well, that was interesting," I said. "She wasn't lying about Jamie, though. She really didn't know why he protested like that. But she *did* lie to you earlier."

"Which part are you talking about?"

"Violet told you she overhead Wesley and Lorelei in the garden. She swore it happened at six. But that's impossible. I heard them arguing by the beautyberry bush, and it was much earlier...probably five. After that, it started to pour, so no one stayed outside."

I'd already told Lance about the way I inadvertently eavesdropped on Wesley and Lorelei yesterday. It happened right before a thundershower sent all of us scrambling for cover.

"Now I remember," he said.

"By six, it was raining buckets. I heard Lorelei yelp, and then they both went inside."

"Did you see the way Violet acted around Lorelei?" Lance asked. "We knew they had their differences, but that was amazing."

I nodded. "I noticed that, too. It's funny, but Violet gets along with the rest of the family. She and Nelle seem quite comfortable together. Nelle even planned to pay for Wesley's funeral expenses, remember?"

"Nothing adds up here," Lance said. "And why did Jamie react so strongly when Mrs. Carmichael bashed Lorelei? For a wedding florist, he seemed awfully concerned about his client."

"I know, right? I've never heard a florist talk that way about one of his brides. As Shakespeare would say, I think he 'doth protest too much.'"

Something stirred behind us then, and a strong voice rang out. "Ah…act three, scene two."

I spun around to find Electra behind me. Like Buck, she'd been drinking, and an empty wineglass dangled from her fingers.

"Excuse me?" I asked.

"You're quoting from *Hamlet*. Act three, scene two." She reached for a bottle from the open bar. "I've played Queen Gertrude a time or two. Now, the real question is…what was the name of the play Hamlet staged for his mother when he said that line? The play-within-a-play?"

"That's easy." Lance didn't hesitate, to my everlasting surprise. "It was called *The Mousetrap*."

I gaped at him for several seconds. Lance and I grew up together in Texas, and he had never, ever quoted Shakespeare to me. Not once. "How in the world did you know that?"

"Hey, I'm cultured." He smiled as he said it, although I detected a hint of defensiveness, too. "I read things."

"Don't get me wrong…I think it's great. I'm all for you becoming more literate. But it doesn't seem like your…your…"

"Your métier," Electra offered. "It doesn't sound like your métier. It means your 'thing.'"

"Thank you," I said. "Your thing. How did you know the name of that play? Tell me the truth, now."

Lance shrugged. "It's also an Agatha Christie play. She got the name from *Hamlet*."

"Okay, now you're mentioning Agatha Christie." I pretended to swoon. "Somewhere in the world, pigs must be flying."

"Very funny," he said. "I told you…I read a lot. And not just books on police procedures. I've been known to pick up a mystery or two."

"Okay, kids. Settle down." Electra seemed amused by our banter. She also reached into the pocket of her sundress to withdraw a long, slim cigarette. "By the way…do either of you have a light?"

We both shook our heads.

"Great. That's just great." She glumly returned the cigarette to her pocket. "Now, about Lance's sudden fascination with Agatha Christie—"

"It's not sudden." Lance jumped in to defend himself. "She wanted to call her play *Three Blind Mice*, but that title was already taken."

"He's right, you know," Electra said. "She only called it *The Mousetrap* because she couldn't have the other title."

The conversation was veering off track, but I welcomed the chance to talk about something—anything—other than a murder investigation for a moment.

"Has anyone seen the play in London?" I asked. "*The Mousetrap?* People say there's nothing like seeing it done with British actors."

"I haven't." Electra shook her head. "Acting doesn't really pay enough for me to go flying off to places like England."

"From what I understand, that's about to change," Lance said. "Pretty soon, you'll have enough money to practically *buy* England."

Electra cut her gaze to me. "You told him? But I said that to you in confidence. I didn't think you'd tell anyone else."

"I tell Lance everything," I said. "And I thought you wouldn't mind."

By the look on her face, she minded very much, thank you.

"It's okay. I won't tell a soul." Lance glanced at me before he made that promise, because we both knew he couldn't keep it. "And it's too bad you never had a chance to tell your stepbrother. Of course, it might not have made any difference."

"Of course." Electra sloshed some red wine into her glass. "I thought the same thing. No matter what, it probably wouldn't have saved my stepbrother."

"And I'm sure your mother is so grateful to have your support this weekend." Maybe I could redirect the conversation and win Electra back to my side. No need to antagonize one of our suspects. "There's nothing like family to help you when you face something horrible."

"That's why I feel terrible about leaving." For once, she sounded sincere. "I wish I could stay, but I have to go back to New York City. My agent got me a reading for a one-woman show. So I booked a last-minute flight that leaves late tonight."

"That must've been a pricey ticket," I said. "Airlines always charge an arm and a leg for last-minute flights."

"It wasn't terrible." She gulped from her wineglass. "And it'll get me there before New York City's even awake. Now, if I could just have my cigarettes with me, I'd be okay. I always get the heebie-jeebies when those planes take off, and nothing calms my nerves like a good smoke."

"Bless your heart," I said. "I'm sure your parents will hate to see you leave Louisiana."

"Oh, I'll be back. They're talking about holding the funeral next weekend. Wesley wanted to be cremated, you know."

"He did?" I squinted. "Well, then, it's a good thing he told your parents that. You know, before he passed away."

"Oh, he didn't tell my parents. He told me. When we…we spoke. A while ago."

"I see." Now it was Lance's turn to look askance. "And just when did you have that conversation with your stepbrother?"

Electra drained the rest of the wine from her glass. "A while ago, like I said. But I'd better scoot now. It'll be time for my flight before you know it."

She quickly turned and left, the click-clack of her heels the only sound in the empty room.

"Well, well, well." I waited for the noise to disappear altogether. "That was interesting."

"Which part? The part where Electra couldn't wait to get out of here or how she's addicted to her cigarettes? She's the only smoker we've met so far."

"Or the only one we know of. And don't forget…the cigarette we found in the cellar was hand-rolled. But Electra smoked Virginia Slims. Unfiltered."

"True." Lance yanked out his notepad and flipped to a specific page. "The cigarette paper we found in the wine cellar was common enough, though. Anyone could buy that brand at Walmart. And she seemed so comfortable with smoking, she very well could know how to hand-roll a cigarette."

"Hmmm. There's something else. How in the world did she find out Wesley wanted to be cremated? She never talked to her stepbrother, and if she did, it's not something you'd bring up in a casual conversation."

Lance nodded. "I thought about that, too. Look, I'm going to go back to the station right now and run a background check on Electra Carmichael. If anything comes up, I'll get an injunction to keep her from leaving."

"Sounds good. You might want to check out her alibi for Friday night, too. She said she didn't fly into Louisiana until this morning. But there's no telling what she was doing when Wesley was murdered."

He suddenly frowned. "By the way…are you okay? You look exhausted. Why don't you go get some rest? I want to run that report anyway, and there's nothing else we can do tonight."

I stiffly stretched my arms over my head. "Now that you mention it, I'm bushed. Maybe I'll stay here tonight, if Nelle has an extra room. I'll bet she does. If not, I can run home and be back here tomorrow morning."

"Thanks for helping me out, Missy. I knew I could count on you." He turned away, his hand already reaching for his cell.

Since everyone else had left by now, I decided to leave, too. I walked down the shadowy corridor, where a few nightlights provided the only illumination, until I reached the kitchen. That was where I spotted Nelle, who was leaning against the doorjamb, which seemed to be her favorite resting spot.

The sounds of pots and pans clanking against each other floated through the open doorway as the caterers closed up shop for the night.

"How're you holding up?" I joined her by the door.

"I'm okay." Despite her reassurances, she looked exhausted. Wispy strands of silver hair fell against her cheeks, and shadows underscored her bright blue eyes.

"What a long day you've had," I said. "Can I help you with anything tonight?"

"Thank you, dear. But I don't think so. Only six people decided to spend the night here, so I have a few bedrooms left. By any chance, would you like one? It's nothing fancy, but I'm sure you'll be comfortable."

Nothing fancy? I stifled a smile. From what I'd seen, everything about the mansion was fancy. Mahogany floorboards, elegant whitewashed furniture, and sky-high ceilings decorated with plaster medallions. The house looked like it belonged in a cover spread for *Southern Living*.

"You're too kind," I said. "And, actually, I'd like to take you up on your offer. I'm so tired, I can barely see straight."

"Why, of course, dear. Let me give you the second bedroom from the stairs. We'll be just down the hall from you, since we let Violet and Foster use our master suite."

At the mention of Wesley's parents, I remembered something else. It was a throwaway comment Nelle had made earlier, but one that stuck with me throughout the day.

"I think it's wonderful you want to pay for Wesley's funeral expenses. A lot of future in-laws wouldn't be that generous."

"Oh, did I mention that? I guess I did. Please do me a favor and keep that to yourself, would you? I daresay my husband wouldn't be pleased if he found out. He wasn't a big fan of our daughter's fiancé. In fact, he counseled her against marrying the boy. She wouldn't listen to him, of course. Children never do."

I nodded sympathetically. "So I've heard. Was your husband worried about Wesley's gambling problem?" While I didn't mean to be indelicate, too much had happened for me not to speak my mind.

"It wasn't just that. He didn't get along with Wesley's father, either. The Carmichaels ran into a bit of financial trouble, and they didn't even offer to pay for the bar at Lorelei's wedding." She leaned closer. "That's usually the groom's responsibility, you know. My husband was afraid the apple wouldn't fall far from the tree. As far as he was concerned, none of the Carmichaels could handle their money."

I cocked my head in surprise. "Really? But what did *you* think of Wesley?"

"I just wanted Lorelei to be happy. That's all. No matter who she married. But listen to me. Here I am, talking your ear off. I should be ashamed of myself for gossiping." She tsked once or twice. "I never could hold my tongue when I'm tired."

"Don't worry. I'm not offended." Truth be told, I found it interesting Wesley's father didn't have enough money to contribute to the wedding. I'd have to call Lance tomorrow morning and share the conversation with him.

At the thought of a phone call, my mind quickly jumped to something else. "Oh, shine!"

"What is it, dear?"

"I forgot to call my fiancé this afternoon. He's probably worried sick about me."

"Then, by all means, call him. Also, there's a linen closet upstairs in the hall. Please help yourself to towels and a washcloth."

"Thank you." I turned on my heels and headed for the stairs. By the time I reached them, I'd already taken out my phone and hit the button for Ambrose's cell. Thankfully, he answered my call on the first ring.

"Where've you been?" He sounded frantic. "I tried to call you, but you didn't answer."

"I'm so sorry, Bo. I turned my ringer to 'mute' during this meeting Lance called. I didn't want to disturb everyone."

"Missy." His voice sounded a warning. "It's nice you didn't want to disturb other people, but you disturbed me. I thought I'd hear from you hours ago."

"I know, I know." Unfortunately, he was right. In my defense, I never meant to leave him hanging. "So much happened this afternoon, I don't even know where to start. But one thing's for sure...I never should've worried you like that. I'm sorry."

"Well..." Fortunately, the warning tone seemed to wane. "You didn't mean to do it, I guess. Just don't leave me in the dark like that. I can't wait until we're married. Maybe then I'll have a better handle on where you are."

"I know, I can't wait either. The day we get married will be the happiest day of my life."

Uh-oh. The wedding. At this rate, my mind was hopscotching from one thought to the other, with no signs of slowing down. "That reminds me,

Bo. I was supposed to call Beatrice this afternoon and ask her about my wedding veil. She stained it by accident, and she was going to try and fix it."

"That's too bad. Are you sure you don't want me to go to your studio and have a look at it? Maybe I can come up with a fix."

In addition to being an excellent designer, Bo possessed an uncanny eye for details. In fact, he wanted to create my whole wedding ensemble, from the gown to the shoes and accessories, but, knowing Bo, I understood the commitment that kind of project would entail, and I knew he wouldn't rest until every detail was perfect.

That's why I insisted on buying a dress off the rack for my nuptials. Any other time of year, I would've been thrilled to wear a custom creation from Ambrose's Allure Couture. But since we'd landed smack-dab in the middle of the wedding season, I couldn't possibly ask that of him. Knowing Bo, he'd work 'round the clock to finish the project, and he needed all his wits about him if he hoped to have a successful summer at his studio.

Unbeknownst to most folks, the vast majority of wedding shops on the Great River Road earned ninety percent of their income during the months of May through September. After that, business fell off to next to nothing, and most shop owners spent their time reordering supplies and handling other administrative tasks.

No, if I let Bo create my wedding ensemble, it would put him in debt because he couldn't take other commissions, and I refused to do that. While he seemed offended at first, he quickly realized I was right and agreed I should buy an off-the-rack ensemble for our wedding day.

And now, the top part of that ensemble teetered in the balance, since Beatrice didn't sound at all sure about her ability to fix the veil in time for the ceremony.

"There's more, Bo," I said. "We still don't have a venue for our reception, or—"

"All right, calm down." He must've sensed the rising panic in my voice. "One thing at a time. You're not going to believe this, but I actually got some good news about our wedding today."

I blinked. "Good news? What's that?" It'd been eons since I'd heard those two precious words.

"I got a call today from Dana, the wedding photographer. She said it was all a big misunderstanding, and she'll be happy to shoot our wedding."

"What? You're kidding!" My joy lasted a full second, until reality set in. "Wait a minute. Is she going to take the pictures, or is her assistant? I can't imagine anyone would want to shoot our wedding when they had the chance to photograph a senator's daughter. Not when there's so much publicity at stake."

"For your information, Dana plans to shoot our wedding herself. Turns out, one of those entertainment magazines wants to cover the senator's event. And they want an 'exclusive' on the wedding pictures."

"That's great!"

"Yep...it looks like we get our photographer back, and Senator Rios gets his picture in *People*. I guess everyone wins."

"Whaddya know." Even though it would've been nice if Dana had done the right thing from the get-go and agreed to photograph our ceremony—even after the senator's office called—I couldn't really blame her. I'd be starry-eyed, too, if someone called and asked me to work for one of the most powerful people in Louisiana. Who was to say I wouldn't have done the very same thing if I'd stood in her shoes?

"Are you sure you're happy about this?" Ambrose asked. "You sound a little subdued."

"No, I'm very happy about it. Thrilled, actually. I'm just tired, that's all. This murder investigation has been brutal. Probably because I feel so bad for Lorelei and her family."

"I get that, but you need to take care of yourself, too. Why don't you call it a night and come back home?"

Ever since Ambrose and I became a couple, we'd been sharing the rental cottage on the outskirts of Bleu Bayou, or what the locals called a "rent house." I loved the charming home. It had bubblegum-pink walls and a garden trellis that brought butterflies right to our front door.

But as much as I wanted to go back home, it didn't seem very safe at the moment. "I don't think it's a good idea for me to drive anywhere tonight. I'm too tired. Would you mind if I spent the night here?"

"Well, I don't know..."

"Before you say more, hear me out. I promised Lance I'd be back at Honeycutt Hall first thing tomorrow morning. It'd save me a step if I could just spend the night here. And it's only for one night. I'll be back home before you know it."

"Then I definitely don't mind. I want you to be safe. Do what you have to do over there and then hurry home. I miss you."

"Ahhh. I miss you, too." The thought of Ambrose leaning against the wall of our kitchen, casually cradling the phone between his strong jaw and his shoulder, like he always did, made me reconsider my decision. "Maybe it wouldn't be so bad if I came home. I could roll down the windows and blast the car stereo—"

"No way." His answer was firm. "You were right the first time. Look, I'll call you in the morning, bright and early, so we can catch up. Now, go get some sleep."

"Thanks, Bo. I love you."

I ended the call and eyed the staircase in front of me. Finally, I could head upstairs and put this day to rest. It already felt like the longest day of my life, and midnight was fast approaching. Didn't they call that the witching hour? Which meant it was a perfect time for me to disappear in a puff of smoke.

Chapter 14

Once I gripped the elaborately carved banister, I began to climb the steps, each one requiring more effort than the last.

The rich wood felt so cool beneath my fingers, and above my head hung more panels of expensive mahogany. According to Nelle, the mansion wasn't fancy. *Rrriiiggghhhttt.* The stairwell alone probably cost more than a month's receipts at Crowning Glory.

Speaking of which, in addition to asking Beatrice about the veil, I was curious about the day's events at my hat shop. While I trusted Beatrice to handle things in my absence, anything could, and usually did, happen at my studio during the wedding season.

One time the studio flooded right before a New York bride's magazine planned to come in and take pictures for a feature story. Another time, I discovered a body in the outbuilding of a historic property I wanted to buy. There was no telling what new crisis I'd face on Monday when I went back to work.

After a few more steps, I heaved myself onto the second-floor landing. The hall was eerily quiet, and nothing stirred behind a line of closed doors that flanked the corridor.

I paused to catch my breath. Nelle had said something about letting me stay in the second bedroom down the hall, but it was the first bedroom that caught my attention. Unlike the others, bright light spilled through the doorway of that one and splashed across the floor like spilled paint.

Being a curious sort, I gingerly made my way to the first room. Although I wanted nothing more than to flop onto the nearest bed and head for dreamland, I couldn't help but peek inside. What if it belonged to Lorelei and I missed the chance to bid her a gentle good night?

I glanced through the doorway and, sure enough, every light inside the room blazed. But it wasn't Lorelei's room, because a men's blazer hung over a straight-backed chair.

I took a step closer, my curiosity still piqued.

Like all the other rooms, this one was richly appointed, with silk shades on the lamps, hand-painted paper on the walls, and a velvet comforter on the four-poster bed. But the comforter looked messy, its folds whorled like the inside of a seashell, as if the lodger had tossed something very heavy on top of it. Not only that, but the door to the closet stood wide open, and a jumble of empty hangers spilled onto the floor. Someone must've been in a terrible hurry; that much was obvious.

I tried to make sense of it all, slowed by the fog that filled my brain. Was the person coming back? From the look of things, the answer was no. I took a step forward, and that was when I noticed a striped bowtie hidden in one of the comforter's folds. And not just any bowtie, either. It was the preppy navy and green tie worn by Buck Liddell at dinner.

Slowly, I backed away from the bed. Then I turned and stumbled down the stairs, my brain trying to play catchup with my feet. I headed for the place where I knew someone would be, and, sure enough, Nelle still leaned against the doorway to the kitchen.

"Mrs. Honeycutt?" I struggled to reach her. "You told me to take the second bedroom down the hall, right?"

She looked surprised to see me. "Yes, dear. Was there a problem with your room?"

"No. That's not it. But who did you give the first room to?"

"The first one?" She pursed her lips. "Let me think. Why…that nice boy who was supposed to be the best man. Buck something-or-other. He told me he was going right to bed, so I'm sure he's fast asleep by now."

Apparently, my expression said otherwise.

"Is something wrong? Isn't he upstairs?"

"No, he's not. His room is empty. He left behind his blazer and a tie, but he's gone."

A feeling of déjà vu washed over me. It reminded me of the scene in the dining room, when Buck disappeared through the exit with the help of two thugs.

"Do you know where he might've gone?" I asked.

"No. Like I said, I thought he'd be in bed by now." Her eyes looked troubled. "I can't imagine where he's gone. He didn't say one word to me about it…"

Her voice trailed off. "My goodness. You don't think he's been kidnapped again, do you?"

I whipped out my cell phone instead of answering. Once I hit the speed dial button for Lance, I willed him to pick up the phone, which he did.

Hallelujah and pass the mustard!

"Hey, there. What're you doing up?" His tone was stern. "I thought you said you were going straight to bed. You need to get some rest, Missy."

"We've got a problem, Lance." I didn't even bother to defend myself. Now wasn't the time or the place for our usual bickering.

"Uh-oh. What's up?"

"I'm afraid Buck's disappeared again. His room is empty."

"Empty? Maybe he's somewhere else in the house. Did you try checking some of the other rooms?"

I shook my head, although he couldn't see me. "I don't need to look around. His clothes are gone, too. Well, most of them. He packed up his suitcase and left."

"You've got to be kidding." Lance softly swore under his breath. "I didn't see that one coming. I'll put out an APB on him. They'll stop him at the airport, if that's where he's gone."

"He's not at the airport." My response came so quickly, it surprised even me. "I think he's heading back to New Orleans. That's where his family lives. That's where *I'd* go if I was in trouble."

"You're probably right. I've got some buddies on the force there. He can't go very far."

"That reminds me of something else." I chewed my lower lip as I struggled to remember the last time I spoke with Buck. It happened when he was trying to hail a car from a ride-share company. "He didn't drive here, Lance. He was trying to call for a car the last time I saw him."

"Good to know. Those companies have their own alert systems, so they can get in touch with their drivers right away. I'll start calling around. Like I said, Buck can't get very far, now that we know he's gone."

"Hey...one more thing." While I knew Lance had work to do, I couldn't control my curiosity. "What did you find out about Electra?"

"Funny you should ask. She has a 'failure to appear' on her record, so I can keep her overnight. My backup will be there in a few minutes to pick her up. If you see her in the hall, make sure she doesn't leave the property."

"How am I supposed to do that?"

"I don't know." He chuckled softly. "But if I know you, you'll think of something."

"Got it. Listen, I'm not sure how much sleep I'm going to get tonight with everything going on. So, feel free to call me anytime if you find out where Buck went. Okay?"

"Maybe. We'll see." He didn't sound very convincing.

"I'm serious, Lance. Don't worry about waking me up. I have a feeling we're getting closer to an answer."

"You and me both. Look, I've gotta get in touch with the ride-share programs. I'll talk to you soon."

With that, he clicked off the line. Whereas before I couldn't wait to drop onto the nearest mattress, now I was much too keyed up to sleep. It looked like my trip to dreamland would have to wait, after all.

Chapter 15

By the time I ended my call with Lance, Nelle had disappeared. She must've returned to the kitchen to pay the caterer while the telephone conversation played out.

It was just as well, since I had more questions than answers at this point. I backtracked to the staircase, where I began to ascend the steps again, my thoughts a million miles away. Just when I reached the halfway point, someone hurtled past me.

Whoosh!

The flash of color disappeared as quickly as it had come.

I spun around, but all I could see was a glimpse of long, red hair. The last tendrils whipped around the corner like dying embers on a match.

"Hey! Electra!"

Now that I knew her identity, I jogged back down the steps. Electra didn't miss a beat, though, and her shoes clattered along the hardwood like a pair of castanets.

I started to call out again, when a loud crash sounded ahead of me. It was followed by two heart-stopping thuds.

I hurried around the corner, where I found Electra splayed on top of the hardwood, her legs pinning Nelle to the wall. The two women were hopelessly tangled, and neither of them moved when I drew close.

"Nelle? Electra?"

I decided to help Nelle first. She closed her eyes as I gently leaned her upright, into a sitting position.

Her pupils fluttered against her eyelids as she struggled to come to. After a second, she opened her eyes. "Wha...what happened?"

"It's okay. You had a fall. A bad fall." Even though it sounded trite, I held up three fingers. "How many fingers do you see?"

She squinted. "Three. I think."

"Good. That's good." I quickly breathed a sigh of relief. She hadn't suffered from double-vision, the talisman of a bad head injury. "How'd you land on the floor?"

"Something hit me on the shoulder." Nelle tried to roll her right shoulder forward, but the pain stopped her. "Ouch."

At that moment, something stirred next to us. It was Electra, who slowly rolled onto her side, which freed Nelle's legs in the process.

"*Uuunnnggghhh,*" she moaned.

I moved over to help her. While Nelle had crashed into the wall, Electra must've landed knees-first on the floor, because thick, red welts appeared on her kneecaps when she rolled over.

I gently cupped my hands under her arms and carefully moved her into a sitting position, like I'd done with Nelle. Now, the two women faced each other in the hall, although neither acknowledged the other.

"How'd I get here?" Electra asked.

"You ran into Nelle, and then you both took a tumble." Although, by the looks of it, Electra sustained the most damage, since her kneecaps flamed bright red.

"I did what?" she asked.

"You ran into Nelle." I jerked my chin toward the other injured party.

"How?"

"You went running through the hall. You two must've met up here, by the kitchen."

"We did?" Electra's eyes widened as the truth set in. "That's awful! I'm so sorry!"

"You didn't mean to do it," I said. "You were both in the wrong place at the wrong time."

"It's okay, dear." Nelle spoke softly. "It could've happened to anyone."

"But I had no right to barrel through your beautiful house like that."

Nelle did her best to smile. "Well, I'm sure you didn't see me standing here. I've told my husband time and time again we need to put more lights in this hall."

"But you've been so gracious to me!" Electra dramatically ran her hand across her forehead, which signaled she was about to perform again. "A pox on my feet! This never would've happened if I'd watched where I was going."

"There, there." Nelle tentatively rubbed her shoulder again. "I don't think anything's broken. Bruised, maybe. Like my pride." She chuckled as she braced her palms on the ground. "It's been years since I sat on this floor. I feel like a kid again."

"Let me help you." I quickly moved to her side.

With a little support, Nelle managed to slowly straighten, and then she rose from the ground. "There. That's better. No harm done."

Electra shook her head as she, too, slowly stood. Once she was upright, she briskly dusted the back of her dress with her hand. She only noticed her knees when she ruffled the hem of the dress.

"Ouch. My knees are going to kill me tomorrow. But at least we cleaned your floor." She managed a smile, too, even with the pain. "It's shinier than it was before. Talk about making a grand exit!"

"Exit?" I asked. "Were you going somewhere?"

The moment I said it, I remembered my promise to Lance. I'd sworn I wouldn't let Electra leave the property, and I wasn't about to go back on my word now.

"I don't think that's a good idea." I spoke quickly, before she could. "You just had a nasty fall. We need to get you water and maybe an aspirin or two."

Thankfully, the distant rumble of a car engine sounded a second later. Lance's backup must've arrived. No one noticed the noise but me, since I was the only one listening for it.

"Well, I was going to leave at first," Electra said. "I had every intention of making my flight so I could audition for the show tomorrow." She quickly glanced at the watch on her wrist. "Actually, the audition is today. It's already past midnight. But then I thought about what you said, Missy. About how much my parents need me here."

"I did?" Funny, but I barely remembered our conversation. Whatever I said, though, it must've made an impression on Electra, because she nodded.

"Yes. You told me I shouldn't leave them alone to face this. It wouldn't be fair."

Well, what do you know? For once, the actress didn't seem to be acting, because she sounded sincere.

"I'm sure they'd love to have you stay," I said. "You'd be a big help."

"I owe it to them. I'm their only living child now."

"So, where were you going when you went running down the hall?" I couldn't imagine what else would prompt her to scurry away like that.

"I actually wanted to find Mrs. Honeycutt here." She cut her gaze to Nelle. "I wanted to see if I could stay in one of the bedrooms upstairs."

"Of course, dear," Nelle said. "We'd love to have you stay with us."

Before anyone else could speak, someone rapped on the front door. The noise startled all of us.

"I'll get it." I dashed from the hall to the foyer, ready to intercept Lance's backup.

Since Electra didn't plan to travel anywhere tonight, we didn't need another police officer.

I unlocked the dead bolt and stepped outside, where I quickly explained the situation to Lance's partner. She returned to the squad car to radio Lance, who must've agreed with me, because the officer started her car again and slowly drove away from the property.

I returned to the house to find the two women still standing in the hall.

"Who was *that* at this time of night?" Nelle cocked her head to one side as she spoke.

"It was Officer LaPorte's backup," I said. "She's returning to the station, though. She just wanted to check with me about something. Look, I don't know about you two, but I'm bushed. I think I'll go to my room and try to get some rest. The morning will be here before we know it."

The group disbanded after that, with Electra and I heading to our rooms, while Nelle returned to the kitchen to speak to the caterers. I ducked into the second bedroom on the right as soon as I reached the upper floor, while Electra headed for the room opposite mine.

I gratefully flopped onto the king-sized bed and willed my heart rate to slow.

Unfortunately, my body didn't listen to me, and I ended up staring at the ceiling for what felt like forever. But only until something else happened.

Chapter 16

When my eyes finally fluttered closed, I felt sleep overtake me. I couldn't have stayed that way for long, though, because something flickered in my periphery, and it caused my eyes to slowly ease open again.

I glanced at the window across the room, where I noticed a soft glow that danced just above the windowsill. An orange glow, which hardened to red around the edges after a moment or two. The light seemed to grow larger as the seconds ticked by, and, by the time I finally threw back the covers and tiptoed to the window, it caused the entire windowpane to glow.

I gazed through the glass, unsure of what I'd find.

There, on the horizon, just past the water tower where Darryl and I discovered Wesley's body, a row of flames licked the night sky. The flames, which rose and fell like a heartbeat on a monitor, spread from a pinpoint of light to about an inch of color, supported by the black horizon underneath.

Something was on fire in the distance, although I had no idea what. I carefully slid the window open and a slight breeze brushed against my cheek as I leaned over the ledge. Just as I'd feared, a fire blazed in the distance, and I heard the crack of dry wood, although that could've been my imagination playing tricks on me.

What should I do? Odds were good no one else would know about the blaze, since everyone else was safely tucked in their beds. Should I call someone? Rouse one of the Honeycutts from their slumber?

As I debated my options, I heard the distinct sound of brittle timbers cracking in two. The noise grew louder and louder as the flames intensified, the fire swallowing everything in its path.

And then it struck me. The *Riverboat Queen*. The beautiful old boat with its ruby-red paint and forest-green trim, which had survived over a hundred years on the river, only to succumb to a fire of dubious origin.

And here it was, burning again. How could someone do that? How could they set fire to the boat, after everything it'd been through? Didn't the ship suffer enough the first time around?

It wasn't right. It deserved better than this! I leaned out the window, prepared to scream for all I was worth, when the noise abruptly stopped. In a final explosion of color, the fire crested twenty feet in the air, until it touched the nighttime clouds.

It's too late. I opened my mouth to scream, but when I did, no sound came out. Instead, I bolted upright in my bed, with sweat coating every inch of my body.

A dream. It was all a dream. But it felt so real. Too real. My gaze flew to the window, which was filled with the black night sky, but nothing else.

If that doesn't beat all. I threw back the covers for real this time and slowly rose. There was no way I was going to be able to sleep after that little adventure, so I groggily made my way to the bathroom and flicked on the light.

A patchwork of wrinkles crimped my sundress like rice paper, so I took it off and steamed it in the bathroom while I quickly showered. Then I splashed cold water on my face and ran a comb through my hair in a feeble attempt to look presentable.

After that, I left the room, grateful to escape the scene of my nightmare, and I headed for the stairs. I only made it a few feet down the hall, though, when something stopped me in my tracks.

Just to be safe, I pinched my arm to make sure I wasn't dreaming again. *Ouch! Nope, wide awake.*

A woman's voice sounded, loud and clear. It was coming from Electra's room, which sat across the hall from mine. Electra sounded angry, and her voice was rough and raw, as if she hadn't slept a wink, either.

She'd left her door open a crack, and light spilled through the space and onto the hardwoods. I didn't move closer, but I didn't need to, since her voice rang out in the quiet.

"I told you this was a big mistake," she said, as clear as day.

She definitely sounded hoarse, too. Not to mention mad. I waited for her companion to say something, but she spoke before the other person could.

"Why didn't I leave? I missed out on my chance. My one chance."

Leaving Honeycutt Hall? I could only imagine that's what she meant.

But, once again, she didn't wait for the other person to speak. Instead, she barreled ahead with her one-sided conversation.

"It was so easy to get rid of him. Almost too easy. Do you think that makes me a bad person?"

My eyes widened. A bad person? If she was speaking about Wesley, which she seemed to be, his murder would make her more than a bad person. She'd be a felon. Who in the world could she be talking to?

I leaned over to see if I could peek into her room, but the only thing I saw was a sliver of lamplight. Maybe if I hopped over the floor to the other side, I'd get a better angle. While I never intended to eavesdrop on yet another conversation, this one was much too interesting for me to stop now.

I waited for the conversation to start up again before I moved.

"We don't have much time now," Electra said. "The end..."

With that, I spun away from the wall—as quickly as my exhausted state would allow—and moved to the other side of the door. I automatically hugged the wall again when I landed there.

Sweet mother of pearl! I couldn't see any more from this position than I could from the last one. Not only that, but now I was farther away from the staircase. What if Electra decided to leave her room and found me eavesdropping on her?

She seemed to be talking nonstop, though, so it was about time for her to pause for breath and let her companion chime in. That might give me a moment to switch back to the other side of the wall, and then I could sneak away before she saw me.

"...always remember you. Don't forget me, either, my love."

My love? Who in the world is in the room with her?

At that moment, the door suddenly jerked open, and my worst fear came true. Electra stepped into the hall, and she frowned when she found me leaning against the wall. "Missy? What are you doing out here?"

I willed my brain to work. Not only was I operating on zero sleep, but I hadn't even had a single cup of coffee to revive me. "Me? Oh...uh...I was going to check on—"

"Were you looking for Mrs. Honeycutt?" She didn't wait for me to finish. "I heard her go downstairs earlier. I think she's probably in the kitchen by now."

Funny, but Electra didn't seem upset about the strained conversation in her room. She sounded a bit tired, but normal otherwise.

"Yes. That's it. I was looking for Mrs. Honeycutt." Hopefully, she wouldn't ask me where I planned to find our hostess, because I had no idea which room she'd stayed in last night. Nelle told me she'd given the master suite to the Carmichaels, but I didn't remember which guest room she planned to sleep in.

"I'll be downstairs in a moment," Electra said. "I have some things to finish up first."

That seemed to be my cue to leave, so I seized on it. I skirted around her, my gaze hungrily seeking out her companion, but she blocked the doorway. So I headed for the staircase instead, before she could ask me any more questions.

Of all the things to hear this morning, I didn't expect a conversation between Electra and her apparent lover to be one of them. Just who was she talking to, and what did she mean when she said it was too easy to get rid of someone else?

I slowly worked my way downstairs, my thoughts sludging around in my brain. I needed to call Lance first thing, so I could tell him what I'd heard. Although I didn't know who Electra was talking to, I could give him the gist of the conversation.

Luckily, I made it to the bottom of the staircase without further incident. I strolled into the kitchen, where a group of people milled about. Among them were Sheridan, the bridesmaid, and Darryl, who once again wore a pair of navy coveralls.

"Good morning." I walked over to Darryl, since he stood next to the coffeepot. Thank goodness, someone had brewed enough Community Coffee to satisfy a herd of houseguests, and I eagerly reached for a Styrofoam cup placed next to the machine.

"Mornin'." He seemed a trifle subdued today. Either Darryl had a lot on his mind, like me, or he wasn't a morning person.

"Everything okay with you?" I filled the cup and took a quick sip of coffee, which was hot and strong, praise the Lord.

"Good 'nuff. Gots ta get some weedin' done today."

"That reminds me." I took another sip, "How'd you find out so much about the plants around here? I know you love gardening, but I didn't think you could memorize every single plant on a property this big."

"'Taint nuthin' to it." He sipped from his cup, too. "I gots to know my herbs for the cook, don' I? And dat one—dat t'orn apple—is tricky. Knew I had ta keep an eye out on dat one."

"Really? How'd you know that?" Seemed to me while Darryl knew everything about growing and propagating the flowers around here, he couldn't be expected to know the chemical makeup of each one. There had to be dozens—if not hundreds—of plants and flowers scattered around Honeycutt Hall.

"Dat jimson weed looks good 'nuf on da outside," he said. "Deys got purple flowers dis time of year. Real pretty. Makes people forget about da poison."

"Officer LaPorte told me all about that. He said Native Americans found out how to numb pain with it, and they used it as a hallucinogen during tribal celebrations. It's funny more people don't know about it."

"It don' grow everywhere. Only down south. Mostly Mexico."

"Well, that makes sense. We're not that far from the border, so I guess birds could've brought it over to this country. I'll have to look for the plant the next time I'm outside."

"Look for sumthin' wit' purple flowers, like da trumpet. Seed pods big an' round. Spiky, too. Den ya know it's da jimson weed."

"Thanks, Darryl." I tossed my cup in the trash, my vision a little clearer now. Although I hadn't slept much last night, maybe I could pretend to be alert this morning.

I was about to make my way to the sunroom when the phone in my pocket suddenly vibrated.

"Hello?" I forgot to check the screen before I answered, so I had no idea who was on the other end.

"Missy? Hi, it's Beatrice."

My shoulders automatically relaxed. Talking with Beatrice always made me feel better, since she was the closest thing I had to a little sister. "Hey there, Bea. What's up?"

"I wanted to tell you as soon as I finished working on your veil."

Uh-oh. I'd forgotten all about the ruined bridal veil. The muscles in my neck began to crimp again at the very thought of it.

"What about the veil?" I couldn't help but sound anxious.

"Don't worry. It came out beautifully. The stain is completely gone."

"Gone?" If I knew rust stains, which I did, they could be harder to erase than red wine.

"Yep. One hundred percent gone. I put it in lemon water, like you suggested. And you were right. You can't even tell some rust ever got on it."

"That's wonderful! Thank you."

"It's the least I could do. I was the one who almost ruined it."

"But you didn't mean to." My relief was palatable. At last, I had a piece of good news instead of one problem after another. Maybe things were starting to turn around for me. Maybe...

"By the way," she quickly added, "yesterday was crazy at the store."

Apparently, I spoke too soon. "Oh, no. Was it a good kind of crazy, or bad?"

"A little of both. Is there any way you can come back to the store today? I'm sure you're busy over there, but it's got to be ten times worse over here."

I mentally ticked through my to-do list. First up, after speaking to Lance, of course, was to take a nice, hot shower. Maybe even brush the tangles out of my hair. Of course, I secretly hoped to nap, but that could be overly optimistic, given everything that was going on around here. "I'll try to get there as soon as I can. But Lance called another meeting this morning. We're getting closer to finding out who killed Wesley Carmichael."

"You're kidding. That's wonderful!"

"Maybe, but maybe not. The best man, Buck, is missing. He's an old college buddy, and they used to gamble together. Not only that, but I overheard his stepsister talking about it, and it didn't sound good."

"That's too bad." Beatrice lowered her voice. "Look, someone's banging at the back door. It must be a delivery. Just get here as quick as you can, okay?"

"Will do." I slowly punched the button on the phone to end the call, and then I returned it to my pocket. Like many things in life, Beatrice's call had brought good news and bad news. She was able to fix my veil, hallelujah, but she sounded desperate for me to get back to the shop. Come to think of it, what was she doing at Crowning Glory so early in the morning? A Sunday morning, no less. I made a mental note to give her a big, fat bonus in her next paycheck, and then I set off down the hall, toward the sunroom.

The first thing I spied when I rounded the corner was a buffet table laden with breakfast food. *Hallelujah and pass the mustard!* Nelle must've convinced the caterers to return, because the table held baskets of bagels, fruit, and beignets.

Nelle stood at the head of the table, next to a stack of Chinet plates.

"Good morning." I hungrily approached the table, momentarily forgetting everything but the sight of those biscuits and butter pats.

"Hello, dear. We sure had an interesting night last night." She chuckled wearily as she passed me a plate.

"You can say that again. And I'm afraid I couldn't sleep much after that. My body was willing, but my mind wouldn't cooperate."

"You and me both."

Only then did I notice blue-black shadows underscored her eyes and deep creases lined her forehead. "Oh, no. You, too?"

She nodded, while I chastised myself for disparaging her appearance. Who was I to talk? I, no doubt, looked like something that'd been "ridden hard and put up wet," as people said in the South. "Maybe we should sit together at the meeting and take a nap when no one's looking."

Her smile waned. "Wouldn't that be lovely? But I have a feeling everyone would notice."

Just then, another person strode up to us. It was Lance, and he looked much too chipper for so early in the morning. "Hi, ho!"

For some reason, the noise echoed through the hall like cannon fire. "Ssshhh. No need to greet the whole house."

"Whoa...what's up with you?" He frowned when he reached me. "Rough night?"

"That obvious, huh? Thanks. Thanks a lot." Nice to know I could count on Lance to make me feel better about my appearance. "You'd look this way, too, if you were up all night."

"Now, I didn't say you look bad." He tried to backtrack as quickly as he could. "It's just that your clothes look a little, uh, lived in."

"Okay, so now I'm 'lived in'? Since when—"

"Hey, kids," Nelle interrupted, "let's play nice. Let's all try to get along this morning, shall we?"

She obviously knows nothing about our relationship. "We *are* playing nice. Lance and I go back twenty years. Trust me, this is as good as it gets."

"Hey, I got something back from the station." Lance wisely decided to change the subject. "The lab analyzed the gift Wesley received." With that, he withdrew a cardboard box from behind his back.

"What is it?" Nelle peered at the package, which looked so ordinary now. It was about the size of a toaster, with no scratches or marks on the box.

"It's something the mailman delivered yesterday," I said. "Darryl intercepted it outside. Someone sent a package to Wesley, and it was a very strange package."

"Oh, dear." Nelle squinted at it again. "Was it meant to be a wedding present?"

"Definitely." Lance balanced the box in his hand, which was no easy feat, considering the weight of the clock case. "They tried to lift some prints off it, but they didn't have any luck."

Since I'd been around Lance and his police investigations for a few years now, I knew exactly what that meant. "So, whoever sent the gift wore gloves."

"Definitely." Lance nodded. "The lab used an aluminum powder on the dark wood, but it came up clean. Same with the powder they used on the glass. Whoever sent the clock knew what he was doing."

"Or she," I reminded him, since more than a few of our cases had involved female criminals.

"Of course." He tucked the box back under his arm. "I'm going to bring this to the meeting this morning. Nothing catches people off guard like visual aids. Maybe I'll get an interesting reaction or two."

"That thing must weigh a ton," I said. "Why don't you set it down and come join me for a bite to eat first? I don't know about you, but I'm starving. I also have something else to talk to you about."

"I think it'd be better if we spoke outside. We'd have more privacy." He glanced at Nelle quickly. "No offense."

"None taken," she said. "I completely understand."

I eyed the buffet longingly, although I knew it was no use. My curiosity wouldn't let me sit back and enjoy a bagel when I had information to discuss with Lance. So I reluctantly handed the plate back to Nelle and made a mental note to grab something to eat later. "Guess I wasn't that hungry anyway."

"Don't worry, dear." She winked at me. "I'll save you some breakfast. We insomniacs have to stick together."

I grudgingly walked away from her and the bountiful breakfast, and then I followed Lance outside. Unlike me, he seemed full of energy this morning. And he looked refreshed, too, dagnabbit. He wore a periwinkle golf shirt and a pair of crisp khakis with knife-sharp pleats. Knowing Lance, he'd stashed a pair of handcuffs in one of the pockets and the ever-present notepad in the other, just in case.

We made a quick detour to the kitchen before we left the house. While I waited by the door, Lance tucked the mysterious gift into a dark corner of the counter, where it wouldn't be noticed. He must've remembered what happened in the wine cellar, though—when someone made off with two pieces of evidence—because he tossed a dish towel over the top, and he even camouflaged the front of it by stacking cups there.

He spoke the minute we stepped outside. "So, you had a rough night?"

"I did. Once I found out we didn't have to worry about Electra leaving, I thought I'd fall right asleep. But I couldn't stop thinking about the case. Or about the *Riverboat Queen*. I had the worst nightmare, but it felt so real."

"I have some more information on that, too," Lance said. "The investigators worked around the clock to see if they could determine how the fire started. Most people don't know this, but they inspected the least-burnt areas first, because that's where the best evidence could be gathered. You'll never guess what they found."

"Besides the motorboat fuel?"

He nodded. "Yes. Someone had taken an O ring out of the fire-suppression system overhead and tossed it in the bathroom. The inspectors found it at the bottom of the toilet bowl, where someone tried to flush it away. Without that O ring, the system didn't work properly, because the carbon dioxide canisters couldn't fire."

"Okay, now you're losing me. I have no idea how that fire stuff works."

"It's pretty simple, actually. People install a fire system at the roofline that sends a retardant through sprayers. But if the carbon dioxide system can't open the canisters of that retardant, nothing gets sent through the sprayers. Nada. Now they're looking at who wanted to burn the boat, and why."

"I hate to say this, but I'm really afraid it might be the riverboat captain. Knowing Christophe d'Aulnay, he wasn't going to let his business go down the drain without putting up a fight."

"You might be right. They're talking to everyone this morning...from the wait staff to the cooks and the d'Aulnays. The boat was insured for up to a million dollars, so there's a lot at stake here."

"Interesting. Also, I wanted to tell you about a conversation I overhead outside of Electra's room."

"What did you hear?" He squinted at me, since neither of us had remembered to bring our sunglasses outside.

"Well, she was talking with someone I couldn't see. But she mentioned how easy it was to get rid of someone. She said it was 'almost too easy.'"

That caught Lance's attention, and his stare hardened. "That doesn't sound good."

"Tell me about it. I couldn't see the other person, but she told him—or her—she wished she would've left the property. And, get this, she said she loved whomever she was talking to. She even called the person, 'my love.'"

Lance whistled softly. "And I didn't see that one coming, either. Now, I know you didn't get a good view, but who do you think she was talking to?"

"Beats me. I wish I would've recorded the conversation on my phone for you. I didn't think quickly enough to do that. She even caught me standing in the hall, but luckily, I bluffed my way out of it."

"Good for you. I'll definitely have to ask her about that this morning. Don't worry, though; I won't tell her where I got my information. And there's one last thing we need to talk about."

I groaned. Already my mind whirled from everything we'd discussed. "Now I know I should've had another cup of coffee. Pretty soon my brains are going to leak out of my ears if I'm not careful."

He chuckled, but he didn't stop. "Got a call around two this morning. My officers picked up Buck. They stopped him at the Louisiana border. You were right. He was trying to get back home to New Orleans."

"I knew it! Out of all the places he could've gone, that one made the most sense to me. But why? Why did he run away from everyone like that?"

"He said he got freaked out when those goons tried to kidnap him. Said he was afraid it would happen again."

"But those two guys are in jail. You said so yourself."

He nodded. "They are. But Buck said he was worried about others. That's not all. He tried to take some stuff from the house with him. I know you told me about the antiques you found on the walkway, but I want to make sure he didn't rob the Honeycutts before he left."

Lance withdrew his cell and lightly touched the screen. "Here, I took some pictures."

Once he accessed the camera function, he tilted the phone at me.

Sure enough, a picture of a beautiful jeweled photo frame appeared. It wore an exquisite border of amethysts, jade, and pearls. I'd recognize it anywhere. The next picture showed an antique candlestick with a burnished HH monogram on the front.

"So, what do you think?" he asked.

"Those are the exact same things he took the first time around." I shrugged, since Nelle didn't seem too bothered by it before. "Mrs. Honeycutt said she gave them to Buck to have them appraised at his father's antiques store."

"That's what he said." Lance frowned. "I don't have a legal reason to keep him at this point. He's got a clean record, and I don't have enough probable cause, let alone reasonable suspicion, to hold him."

"What's going to happen to him, then?"

"First thing I want to do is get him back to the house," Lance said. "I want everybody in the room when we meet this morning at seven." He hit a different button on the cell's screen. "I'll call the station and ask them to transfer him here."

While Lance called his counterparts at the police station, I studied the grounds around me. Sure enough, a thornberry bush appeared among a cluster of azaleas and asters. The flowers were shaped like miniature trumpets, just as Darryl described them, with dark purple centers and lilac tips. The seed pods were larger than I thought they'd be—about the size of a lime—with barbs that resembled spikes on a puffer fish.

Such a strange, alien seed pod for such a pretty plant. Other than that, the thornberry bush looked like its neighbors, with the same veined leaves and hardy stalks.

Once Lance finished with his call, he slipped the phone back in his pocket.

"What happened?" I asked.

"Nothing. My partner's bringing him back here. Other than that, I'm afraid we're at a standstill."

"So, what're you going to say to everyone this morning? Do you still want to go through with the meeting?"

"Definitely." He studied the ground, too, but his thoughts seemed a million miles away. "I bet you weren't the only one who couldn't sleep last night. People get loose-lipped whenever they're tired, and I'm going to use that to my advantage this morning. Let the tension build until someone cracks."

"Sounds like you've been talking to Electra," I said. "Like you're going to put on a show for us."

"I just might," he said. "And according to my calculations, it's show time."

We slowly turned around. Someone inside the house in front of us knew more about the murder than he—or she—was saying. And it was time to find out who.

Chapter 17

Lance strode back to the kitchen, with me on his heels. By the time we stepped into the room, several people had bunched around the coffee machine, groggily waiting for a turn with it.

Nelle was there, since most of her guests had gravitated to the kitchen instead of the sunroom, and Lance quickly moved to her side. He whipped out his cell and scrolled through the pictures for her, and, just like I thought, she seemed nonplussed by them. She shook her head a few times, until Lance finally lowered the phone.

"So, we meet again."

A voice sounded behind me, and I turned to see Electra. She still sounded groggy, and her dress looked about as wrinkled as mine.

Hopefully, she had no idea what I overheard in the hall. "So, how was your night?"

"Not the best," she said. "I couldn't sleep a wink. The suspense is killing me."

"I'll bet." *Wonder what she'll say when Lance confronts everyone this morning?* "You sound like you haven't had any coffee yet. Let's go get you a cup."

Since Lance was busy with Nelle, and I wanted to ask Electra a few questions, I led her over to the coffeepot. Luckily, there was still some left, so I reached for it before anyone else could grab it. "Here you go." I quickly poured some coffee into a cup and passed it to her. "Anything interesting happen this morning?"

Her eyes narrowed. "Interesting? It's only seven in the morning. About the most interesting thing to happen to me has been this coffee."

"What I meant was, have you had a chance to talk with anyone yet today?"

"Me? I don't think so." She frowned as she took a sip from her cup. "That's kind of a strange question, don't you think?"

"Just making conversation." Maybe if I played it off, she wouldn't suspect the real reason for the question.

"Well, this weekend has me so frazzled, I can only imagine how it's affected my mom and stepdad."

At the mention of Electra's parents, my gaze flitted around the room, to the others. It seemed everyone had found their way downstairs, to the kitchen, except for the Carmichaels. Over there, by the sink, stood Jamie Lee, with Lorelei next to him. He'd turned his back on the group as he spoke with her, and he nervously shifted his weight from one foot to the other.

At the other end of the sink stood Stormie, who looked camera-ready this morning in a crimson suit with a form-fitting jacket. Leave it to Stormie to wear a tight jacket, even while pregnant. Sure enough, the jacket struggled to close at the bottom, and she hadn't bothered to fasten the last few buttons.

Come to think of it, what was Stormie doing in the kitchen with us? Ever since Darryl and I discovered Wesley's body in the water tower, people hadn't exactly welcomed her presence. They could tolerate her when they thought she planned to film a puff piece about the "wedding of the century," but now that her had story changed into a hard-hitting news piece about a murder investigation, she didn't really belong here. Not with the victim's family so close by. I had half a mind to tell her that, since Nelle would be too polite to say it, and everyone else would be too intimidated.

Since she wasn't bothering anyone at the moment, though, and I still hoped Electra might slip and mention her early-morning visitor, I decided to keep my mouth shut.

At that moment, Electra pointed to something on the counter. While still tucked out of sight, someone had ripped open the cardboard box Lance left there. My heart immediately fell to my stomach. *Not again.*

I closed my eyes, willing the clock to be there. Sure enough, when I opened them again, I spied it at a different spot on the counter. *Gracious light*! We couldn't afford to have another piece of evidence go missing, and that was too close for comfort.

"What is that?" Electra asked.

"It's a gift someone sent your stepbrother. It arrived yesterday."

"But what is it?" When she squinted, I realized she couldn't see it as well as I could.

"It's an old clock. It's an antique, actually. Very pretty." I left off the part about the cryptic message on the back.

"You don't say." She glanced back at the coffeepot. "Maybe I should take some of this upstairs to my mom. She might need the caffeine this morning, too."

"That's a good idea. Be sure to come down to the sunroom afterward."

Just as Electra reached for the stack of cups, a noise stopped her short. The back door banged open, and who should enter the room but Buck, with his head hung low and his gaze glued to the floor.

Everyone fell silent. Close on his heels was Lance's partner, the pretty Hispanic I'd already seen several times this weekend.

"Hey, y'all." He mumbled the greeting as he shuffled into the kitchen.

"Thanks for giving him a ride, Leticia," Lance called to her. "No need to stay. I can handle it from here."

His partner nodded, and then she worked her way back to the exit. In the meantime, Buck ignored Lance and headed over to where I stood.

"You're back," I said, unnecessarily.

"Looks like it." He nodded at the coffee machine. "Mind if I get some?"

"Suit yourself." I moved aside so he could reach it.

"Where did you go?" Electra asked. "We all thought you were hiding something because otherwise you would've stayed here. It wasn't very smart of you to run away, to tell you the truth."

Look who's talking, I wanted to say, but that would only let her know I was on to her.

Her comment didn't seem to faze Buck. "I had some business back in New Orleans. Thought I'd get a jump on it, since it wasn't doing me any good to stay here."

"Oh, come on." Electra didn't appear to be buying it. "That's baloney. First, two guys who look like they came straight out of central casting for the Mafia showed up on the doorstep and hustled you out of here. Then you packed your bags and ran away in the middle of the night. That doesn't sound like a little side trip to visit the folks, if you know what I mean."

"Okay. Maybe you're right. To be honest, I was scared. I thought if I stayed here, the bookie would send someone else to get me. Wesley owed him a lot of money, and those guys don't exactly play nice, if you know what I mean."

I plucked a coffee cup from the stack and handed it to him. Listening to these two could prove mighty interesting. "Here. Sounds like you might need this."

He nodded his thanks and stepped up to the machine. While he got some coffee, I quickly scanned the crowd for Lance. He and Nelle still stood side by side, next to the door, and they'd obviously finished their conversation. It seemed the perfect time to get the ball rolling.

"C'mon, you guys," I said. "Detective LaPorte is giving us an update on the case in the sunroom. Why don't we head over there now?"

Buck took a big gulp of coffee, and then he walked over to the sink and poured the rest down the drain. "No problem. This coffee isn't exactly worth sticking around for."

He turned to throw away the cup, when something on the counter caught his eye. He gravitated toward the clock, which lay on its side, with the dish towel nearby.

"What's this?" He pointed at the gift.

"Just something that was sent to the house yesterday," I said. "Look, we should probably get going—"

"What a beauty." He seemed mesmerized by it. "Look at that wood."

Before he could reach for it, and possibly contaminate the evidence, I plucked up the dish towel and threw it over the wood.

"Here...you need to use that if you're going to touch it," I said. "And you'll notice someone ruined the back of it with a black felt pen."

"Why would anyone do that?" He looked pained by the thought. "Don't they know it's an antique?"

"They wrote something on the back?" Electra edged closer. "Let me see."

I carefully gripped the bottom of the case with the towel and gently turned it over. The minute the graffiti appeared, Electra gasped.

"That's awful! I can't imagine what someone was thinking. Is that supposed to be a joke?"

"Hardly." I carefully turned the clock around again and laid it on the counter.

"Even with the writing, the clock is priceless," Buck said. "It's from Asia. China, to be exact. Probably produced in a place called Nanjing. I'd put the date at about eighteen hundred."

"You can tell all that from one look?" I asked.

"Sure. The case tells me everything I need to know. It's made of rosewood, which looks a lot like mahogany. And the scrolled base is typical for that period. See the slit on the bottom? It's actually a drawer, to hold the winding keys."

He took the towel from me and slid open a hidden compartment at the base of the clock. Sure enough, two miniature brass keys twinkled.

"Cool!" Electra breathed the word. "Amazing no one lost the keys after so many years."

"It probably stayed in the same family," Buck said. "But that's not what gets me. The real question is this: why would anyone send a clock to a wedding in the first place?"

"What do you mean?" I asked. "Because it looks like a family heirloom?"

"Well, there's that," he slid the compartment closed again. "But there's more to it than that. No one in China would ever give a clock for a wedding gift, because it's supposed to be bad luck. The word 'clock' in Mandarin is the same word for 'the end.' So it's considered a bad omen to give a new couple a clock. Everyone knows that."

I blinked. And, all at once, the words hit home. The truth almost blindsided me when I realized what he'd said.

Chapter 18

"I…I have to go." I stumbled away from the counter, almost knocking into Buck in the process.

A million thoughts raced through my mind. Of course, Buck and Electra stared at me as if I'd gone crazy, but I couldn't very well worry about that right now. There'd be time enough to explain everything *after* we caught the murderer.

I hurried toward the door, and, thank goodness, Lance still stood beside it. He hadn't moved from his spot with Nelle, but his smile waned when he saw me.

"Missy? What's wrong?"

"You have to come with me." I quickly glanced at Nelle, who didn't seem to know what to make of my breathless announcement. "Now."

There was no time to lose. So I grabbed his arm and practically pulled him into the foyer.

"Whoa there, Missy." He dug in his heels by the front door. "What's all this about?"

"I know who killed Wesley. It's Jamie, the florist. He's the one who sent the clock. He must've been the one who poisoned the groom Friday night."

To his everlasting credit, Lance didn't laugh at me. Instead, he turned on his heels and hurried back to the kitchen, as fast as he could.

I scurried behind him, suddenly energized by the latest turn of events. It all seemed so logical now. If only we'd known what to look for in the beginning.

Lance hurried back to where Nelle stood. "Mrs. Honeycutt." He quickly spun her around. "Did Jamie Lee spend the night here last night?"

"Why, yes. Yes, he did." The intensity of his voice surprised her. "Why, Officer? Is there a problem?"

"Just answer me this: where did he sleep?"

Her gaze pinballed to me, but I remained silent. "Why, I think he took the last bedroom down the hall. He wanted to leave, but Lorelei wouldn't let him go."

With that, Lance released her arm and broke into a dead run. I struggled to keep up with him, my heart pounding inside my chest. I tried to ignore the faces watching us as we raced down the hall, the figures blurring from one person to the next by the time we reached the staircase.

Lance flew up the steps, his long legs hurdling them two at a time. I hopscotched from one to the next, but he still outpaced me.

I finally pulled even with him when he paused by the door to the last bedroom, clearly winded.

I let him walk into the room first, after a few deep breaths, where he drew his gun. When he reached the center of the room, he slowly turned around and around. After a moment, he waved me inside.

The room was a mess. The dresser's drawers hung open, papers littered an antique desk, and a braided rug was folded up against the wall like a flattened accordion. A large four-poster bed dominated the room, just like Buck's, only the comforter on this one laid in a heap and pillows spilled over the sides.

Lance turned around again. "Looks like we missed him."

"But...but that can't be." I tried to focus, even with the adrenaline coursing through my veins. Across the way, someone had thrown open the closet door, and hangers tumbled off the rod, every which way. Nothing had been left behind. Nothing, that was, but the scent of something vaguely familiar.

"We just missed him, Lance. He can't be but a few seconds ahead of us."

"How do you know that?" he asked.

"Smell the air. It's his cologne."

We both turned and dashed from the room. This time, I took the lead, as we flew down the stairs and into the foyer. By now, everyone else in the house knew something was afoot, because they all congregated by the front door.

"Out of my way!" I threaded through the throng and yanked open the door. Once I jogged down the outer staircase, I finally paused on the last step to wait for Lance.

Nothing else stirred around me. "C'mon, Lance," I yelled. "He must've gone around back!"

I sped along the side of the mansion, skirting around one of the water towers. Once I moved past the wine cellar where I'd first discovered the used glasses and cigarette paper Friday night, I continued onto the garden path. It was here that a rainstorm had forced me to seek shelter. And it was here where I once again heard the sound of voices as I drew near the beautyberry bush.

I thrust out my arm to stop Lance. Luckily, he skidded to a stop, only seconds from crashing into the bush.

Someone spoke on the other side of it, just as we arrived.

"We have to get out of here." It was a man, and he sounded desperate.

The branches blocked me from seeing the speaker, but I recognized the voice right away.

"It's Jamie," I whispered.

"Are you sure?"

"Yes." Luckily, the unmistakable scent of Paco Rabanne drifted on the air, unimpeded by the flowers on the bush, which wouldn't bloom for another month or so. "I'd recognize that cologne anywhere."

Sure enough, Jamie spoke again. "Come with me. You know you want to. You know you love me."

Love me? Lance and I exchanged quick looks. Everything else fell silent in that moment; even the insects, which seemed to know something was up.

"I can't." Now a woman spoke.

"Oh, my gosh," I whispered. "It's Lorelei."

"That can't be right," Lance whispered back.

"It is." While I didn't want to be the bearer of bad news, we had to face facts. "That's our bride, Lance."

Apparently, Jamie didn't take Lorelei's rejection lightly. When he spoke, his voice was raw. "You can't stay here. I won't let you."

"I don't have a choice," she said. "Don't you see that? Otherwise, they'll think I had something to do with it."

"But didn't you? You were the one who suggested the poison."

"I didn't think you'd actually go through with it," she scoffed. "I thought you'd drug him just enough so he'd miss the ceremony."

"Miss the ceremony?" Now it was Jamie's turn to scoff. "What good would *that* do? He was never going to let you go. You have to believe me."

I pried aside a branch to see the couple. Lorelei stood across from Jamie, her arms folded tightly across her chest.

"No." She shook her head. "I won't go with you."

Suddenly, Jamie lurched forward and grabbed her wrist.

"Come with me." His voice had hardened. "It's not a question, Lorelei."

"What are you doing? You're hurting me. Let me go!"

Lance must've heard enough, because he barreled around the hedge, until he emerged on the other side. Everything slowed at that point. I cautiously followed behind him, but only close enough to watch the action without getting in Lance's way.

Rage contorted Jamie's face. Before he could react, Lance dove into him and tackled him to the ground. He had no choice but to release Lorelei's wrist at that point, and the girl's arm jerked backward.

It was no contest. Not only did Lance outweigh Jamie by at least forty pounds, but he had hundreds of hours of police training under his belt. He expertly wrestled Jamie onto his stomach, and then he pressed his knee into the small of the man's back.

In one fluid motion, Lance retrieved a pair of handcuffs from his back pocket and flicked them up so the blades pointed toward Jamie's wrists. He clicked the shackles into place, and then he yanked on the chain between the man's hands to make sure the blades had engaged.

Everything was over in a matter of seconds.

"You have the right to remain silent…" Lance began.

At that point, I brought my gaze to Lorelei, who'd stepped several feet away from the melee.

I expected her to look horrified. To gape at the two men struggling only six feet away. But instead, a slight smile played on her lips, as if she knew what was going to happen even before it did. As if she *wanted* it to happen.

"Lance!" I yelled.

But he couldn't hear me. He was too busy reading Jamie his Miranda rights while he pinned the man to the ground.

So I did the first thing that popped into my head. I lurched toward Lorelei and grabbed her arm before she could leave.

"Let me go!" she hissed.

"Not so fast." I tightened my grip, until my knuckles blanched white against her arm. "You knew all along. Didn't you? You knew Jamie was going to kill Wesley."

"You're crazy," she spat. "I don't know what you're talking about."

By this time, Lance had finished reading Jamie his rights, but he kept his knee planted squarely in the middle of the man's back, just in case.

"Lance!" I only hoped he could hear me now.

He finally brought his gaze to mine. His demeanor changed when he saw Lorelei struggle against me. "What's going on?"

"Don't forget about this one," I said. "She knew all along."

At that moment, Lorelei did something shocking. Instead of denying it, like I expected, she began to laugh. But not a normal laugh. It sounded high-pitched and mildly hysterical. It was the laugh of someone who had nothing left to lose. "What a joke. You can't prove anything. And I'm not saying a word till my attorney gets here. He's going to destroy you two."

Slowly but surely, Lance rose from the ground, and then he yanked Jamie up about a foot. Dust coated the man's face, and he'd closed his eyes.

"Here." Lance nodded at me. "You hold onto this one. Good thing I brought a zip tie."

He and I traded places while he pulled a plastic cable tie—what police called a flex-cuff—from the pocket of his shirt. Leave it to Lance to be prepared for anything, because he quickly used the tie to secure Lorelei's wrists.

By now, I knew the proper way to maintain control of a subject—thanks to the half-dozen times I'd already helped Lance with a police investigation—and Jamie didn't put up much of a fight. He'd sunk back to the ground, and he could feel the pressure of my knee against his back. He knew he couldn't escape.

When Lance finished subduing Lorelei, he roughly pushed her forward. "We're going to take a little walk. There's a houseful of people who would love to know what's going on around here."

Chapter 19

Once Jamie rose as well, we all began to walk single file toward the house. Jamie and Lorelei resembled prisoners on a forced march—which they were—and they hung their heads as they shuffled along. Neither said a word, and they didn't resist when Lance and I guided them onto the front steps.

By now, the entire household had emptied onto the front porch. Over there was Darryl, who held his gardening shears like a pistol, just in case. Beside him stood Stormie, who looked so surprised, she forgot to use the microphone at her side.

The only one who didn't look dazed was Nelle, and only because she seemed horrified instead. She gaped at us as we slowly straggled up the steps. When her daughter finally stood within arms' reach, she leaned forward and spoke directly to her. "Lorelei? What's going on? What—"

"I'm afraid you're looking at the people who killed Wesley Carmichael," Lance interrupted. "Jamie here administered the poison, but Lorelei was his accomplice."

"I...I don't understand." Nelle's gaze shifted to me. "Lorelei had something to do with this?"

"I'm afraid so," I said. "She tricked Jamie into committing the murder. They were a couple all along."

Something rustled nearby, and, before anyone could stop her, Violet burst forward. She reared back her hand as soon as she reached Lorelei, and then she struck the girl as hard as she could. The slap echoed in the stillness, and Lorelei's head snapped back.

When Violet moved to do it again, Darryl rushed forward and grabbed her hand in midair. He held it there, immobile, while Violet shook with rage.

"I knew it! I knew she had something to do with it. Why, I'll...I'll..."

Before she could finish, Darryl wrapped his arm around her shoulders and pulled her away from Lorelei. She kicked and sputtered, but Darryl somehow managed to maneuver her back to the front door, where he pulled her into the house, and the duo disappeared.

We were all too stunned to speak.

Nelle recovered first, and when she did, she shook her head sadly. "Why, Lorelei? Why would you do that?"

Slowly, Lorelei's head tilted up. An angry red welt traveled from her jawline to her ear. The blow seemed to have taken away some of her fight, but not all of it. "Daddy always told me I could do better. He knew I deserved more than Wesley."

"But Wesley loved you, honey." Nelle slowly but surely leaned away from her daughter, as if she was seeing the girl in a new light. And it wasn't a pretty picture. "But you cheated on him, didn't you? I didn't raise you that way. What happened?"

"I grew up." Bitterness tinged Lorelei's voice. "And I almost gave you the perfect wedding. Isn't that what you wanted, Mother? Sorry to disappoint you, but I wasn't going to spend the rest of my life in debt."

The words stunned Nelle. But after a moment she recovered enough to turn her back on her daughter. She began to walk away slowly, and she never once looked back as she, too, disappeared through the front doorway.

In the meantime, Lance must've realized the show was over, because he pulled Lorelei in front of him and began to guide her up the steps. The crowd cut them a wide swath, and I followed in their wake, with Jamie in tow.

I suspected which path Lance would take, and, sure enough, he moved through the foyer and into the hall. The sunroom beckoned at the very end of it, and we once again found ourselves just outside the sunny room.

By now, I wanted no part of the breakfast buffet, and I marched past it with Jamie at my side. The wedding party must've felt the same way because they, too, bypassed the table on their way to the sunroom.

But Lance stopped the group before anyone could enter. "I'm sorry, but everyone else can go home now. I don't need to conduct any more interviews. Thank you all for cooperating, and I'm sure you'll read about the arrest in your local paper."

"Um, hm." Stormie cleared her throat pointedly and indicated the microphone at her side.

"Or check out the local TV newscast," he added. "I'm sure Miss Lanai here will cover everything on the six o'clock news."

The way Stormie beamed at that, she looked like the proverbial cat who'd just swallowed the canary. Despite the ugly scene on the porch, she seemed to enjoy every moment of it.

Chapter 20

One by one, the group began to disperse. Some people went upstairs to gather their things, while others headed directly for their cars. Within a few minutes, only Electra and Darryl remained with us by the sunroom.

Lance nudged Lorelei ahead of him, and I followed suit with Jamie. My charge didn't need any coaxing on where to sit, because he flopped onto the wicker settee as soon as he entered the room, and then he leaned his head against the backrest.

Once Lance read Lorelei her Miranda rights, he moved her to one of the wicker chairs, too, but she defiantly perched on its armrest.

"We're taking you down to the station in a few minutes," he said, "but I want to get a few things straight first. Is there anything either of you want to tell me?"

He didn't elaborate, but that was part of his plan. The less Lance said the better, because most suspects couldn't cope with silence for more than a few seconds. Maybe it was the guilt that spurred them on, but I'd seen criminals crack after just a moment or two. As if they needed a distraction—any distraction—from what they'd done.

"I'm not saying anything." Lorelei kept her gaze trained on the ceiling. "And you can't make me."

"It's true, I can't." Lance modulated his voice to make it sound as if the conversation was nothing more than an ordinary, everyday chat. "But why don't you help yourself by telling me what you know. The judge might go easier on you if he hears you were cooperative."

When no one spoke, Lance repeated his offer. "That's what I'd do, if I were you. Tell me what you know. Don't leave anything out. It's all going to come out anyway."

When Jamie moved to speak, Lorelei jerked her head down. "Don't you dare," she hissed at him. "It's a trap. He's trying to get us to confess. That's what you're doing, isn't it, Detective?"

"Call it whatever you want, but I'd call it a little conversation. Just the four of us." He threw me a look, which was my cue to get involved.

"I'm sure you're both worried sick about this," I said. "Maybe it was an accident. Maybe you didn't know the poison was going to kill Wesley. I could see how that would happen."

Of course, I knew no such thing, but if Lance was going to be the big, bad police detective, I was going to be the sympathetic sidekick. There was a reason the good cop/bad cop routine was so cliché, and that was because it worked.

"That's ... that's it!" Jamie gazed at me hopefully. "You understand. I only gave him the cigarette because I thought it'd make him feel better. You know, doctor it up with something that would help him."

"Jamie!" Lorelei's voice was icy. "Shut up. Don't say another word. I'm warning you."

"Or what?" Compared to her, his voice was soft. "You'll leave me? I already know that's going to happen. What else can go wrong?"

"A lot." She wasn't swayed by his tone. "Don't say another word until I call my attorney. I mean it."

Jamie slowly shook his head. "No. I'm not going to listen to you anymore. You're the one who's been trying to trick me. This is all your fault."

"Oh, grow up," she said. "I didn't make you do anything you didn't want to do."

"Sounds to be me like you might've been a victim here, too, Jamie." I used my most sympathetic tone. "It happens sometimes, you know."

"Yes. Yes, it does." Once again, his gaze was pleading. "She's the one who told me I should use the thorn apple after we both read about the plant. I thought it was interesting when I found out what it could do. But she took it one step further. She's the one who bought the cigarette papers. She's the one—"

"For the last time, Jamie, shut up!" Lorelei spoke through clenched teeth. She looked like she wanted to strike him, but the handcuffs wouldn't let her.

Finally, he seemed to realize he couldn't win, because Jamie dropped his head and fell silent.

Which was Lance's cue to pull out his cell phone. Once he dialed a number and said a few words into the receiver, he lowered it again. "Now, we wait."

While I leaned against one of the walls, grateful for the support for my aching back, Electra approached me cautiously. Like me, she looked like something a cat had dragged in, as my grandfather would say, and she barely managed a weak grin.

"What a relief!" She joined me on the wall, our shoulders nearly touching.

"You can say that again." The words sparked a memory, and I instantly turned toward her. "That reminds me…I overheard something this morning, out in the hall."

Lance noticed us talking, but he kept one arm locked on Lorelei, and the other on Jamie.

"Really?" she said. "I thought I heard a noise out there. I figured someone was pacing the hall, and when I found you out there, I assumed it was you."

"Nope. I heard you arguing with someone, so I stopped by your door."

"Sounds to me like you were eavesdropping." Her tone was more teasing than angry, hallelujah. "I don't care about that. But what did you hear?"

"You said you had gotten rid of someone, and it sounded like you were bragging about it."

At that point, she actually laughed. It sounded dry and hoarse, but it was a laugh, nonetheless. "You know what you overheard, right?"

Yep, she was definitely laughing at me, although I had no idea why.

"I thought maybe you were confessing to the murder," I said. "Maybe talking to your accomplice."

"Ha!" That brought another bark of laughter, and even Lance looked taken aback by it.

"What's going on over there?" he asked.

"I was telling Electra here about a conversation I overheard. I actually thought she was going to confess to the murder. Only she sounds the least bit contrite about it."

"That's because I was running lines for a play." She must've decided it was time to come clean, because she quickly sobered up. "It's that new play I was telling you about. The one my agent wanted me to audition for in New York City."

"But I thought the audition was today."

She had mentioned something about taking the late flight so she wouldn't miss it.

"It *was* today," she said. "But it turned out the producers couldn't make it, either, so it got rescheduled to tomorrow. I was practicing in my room. That's what you overheard."

"A play?" Although perfectly plausible, I still felt confused. "Do you always run lines by yourself?"

"No, not normally, but I didn't have anyone else to read them with. I wasn't about to wake someone up and ask them to do me a favor."

"Ah ha." Looking back, the explanation made perfect sense. "Well, now I feel foolish."

"Don't," she said. "You were just worried about finding the right person. The person who killed my stepbrother. How can I be mad about that?"

"You can't," Lance agreed. "Until this morning, several people qualified as suspects in the case."

"It looks like you don't have to worry about it anymore." She indicated Lorelei and Jamie with a sweep of her hand. "Looks like you figured it out. So, thank you. I feel a lot better about leaving town now that we know who killed Wesley."

At that moment, a siren sounded in the distance. The sound drew closer and closer until it was joined by the crunch of tires on the pebbly drive.

"Well, I guess I'd better go," Electra said. "Thanks again. For everything."

With that, she disappeared, and she was replaced by four uniformed police officers, who rushed into the room. Two of them surrounded Jamie. He'd closed his eyes earlier, and it was hard to know whether he was sleeping now, or praying. My guess was a little of both, because the officers had to practically carry him from the sunroom.

Lorelei was a different story. She stood ramrod straight, and then she walked stiff-legged out of the sunroom. There was no telling what was going through her head, and, to be honest, I didn't care.

As soon as the officers muscled Lorelei from the room, Lance turned to face me. "You okay?"

"I feel great, actually. I feel sorry for Wesley's parents—Lorelei's, too—but it feels good to finally get at the truth."

He nodded. "That's how I always feel at the end of a case. It's like a breath of fresh air when the lid comes off the secrets. Do you want to come down to the station with me?"

"I'd like to, but I can't." I quickly scanned the room for a clock, which I found hanging by one of the windows. The hands stood at twelve and nine, which meant several hours had passed since Beatrice's phone call. Even though we didn't open the studio until noon on Sundays during the wedding season, there was no telling how many clients had pestered her by now.

"I need to get back to my studio," I explained. "Sounds like Beatrice has her hands full. You know, we're right in the middle of the wedding season, so it's all hands on deck."

"I understand. Thanks again for all your help this weekend."

"Call me later, okay? Let me know what happens during the interviews. I have a feeling Lorelei's going to crack, too. She can't keep quiet for too much longer."

"I hope you're right." He checked the time as well. "I'd better hustle if I want to seal off the bedrooms upstairs and then get to the station. There's no telling what the suspects left behind here."

His words automatically piqued my curiosity. "You mean you're going to search their bedrooms? Hmmm. Maybe I can spare a few minutes."

Truth be told, I enjoyed watching Lance comb through a suspect's room. It was like watching a choreographer piece together a dramatic new dance. One step would lead to the next, and then all the steps would culminate in one knockout finish.

"You can tag along." He smiled broadly. "Like they say in Texas, it won't be your first rodeo."

Chapter 21

Lance and I moved to the exit, but we didn't get very far. Standing just outside the door was Violet, and she seemed much calmer than before. She even gave me a shy smile as she approached.

"I was hoping to talk to you."

"We're in hurry." Lance barely slowed his pace. "Can it wait?"

"I meant Miss DuBois, actually."

I pulled up short. "You know, anything you say to me, you can say to Detective LaPorte here. He's the police officer, not me."

My, that feels good. Usually, Lance had to talk people into letting me join a conversation, but now I had a chance to repay the favor.

"Okay, then," she said. "If you insist."

"I do. We're a team."

"Well, that's what I wanted to talk to you about." She nervously toyed with a thread that dangled from the sleeve of her blouse. "I'm afraid I owe you both an apology."

"An apology?"

"Yes. I didn't help either one of you very much. In fact, I might've gotten in the way. But you need to understand something. If I lost my husband and my son, it would just kill me. I didn't want Foster to get any more tangled up in this mess than he already was."

"What made you think you were going to lose Mr. Carmichael?" While I didn't understand it, she sincerely believed every word, because worry etched her face.

"My husband loaned a lot of money to Wesley over the years. Even when he found out about the gambling. I thought if you knew that, Foster might get in trouble, too."

"But it's not illegal to loan someone money," Lance said.

"No, but it's not right when that person has an addiction, like Wesley did. I thought you'd charge Foster for it."

"I don't think that's possible." I shot a quick glance at Lance, who confirmed my suspicion with a nod. "No one's going to charge your husband with anything."

"That's so good to know. My husband never did things like that before. He used to make better decisions. Wonderful decisions. But ever since he started drinking again, everything changed."

I bit my tongue, because I'd suspected as much. No one reeked of alcohol at eleven in the morning unless he had a serious problem with it.

"You've had a lot to deal with, Mrs. Carmichael." I spoke gently, since this woman obviously had been through a lot. "Are you going to be okay?"

She nodded. "I think so. My daughter invited me to come stay with her in New York City for a while. Just until things calm down."

"That's probably a good idea." While I didn't know enough about the Carmichaels' marriage to offer any input, it seemed Violet needed to get away for a while. And Electra seemed to have enough chutzpah for both of them. She could take care of her mother now, instead of the other way around.

"Well, I guess that's all," Violet said. Already her thoughts seemed a million miles away. "Thank you for everything."

She turned and slowly retreated down the hall, her footsteps as halting as her speech had been.

"Well, that was interesting." I waited for her to disappear before I spoke.

"I'll say. It obviously made her feel better to get that off her chest."

"I don't know why she confided in me." I threw him another look. "Somehow, people can't stop themselves from telling me their secrets. It must be my kind face."

"Sure, that's it. You and your kind face." He threw me a playful punch. "Well, as long as you haul that kind face of yours upstairs to help me out, I won't disagree."

Before I could reply, he headed for the stairs, so I joined him. We climbed the steps in tandem, since the wide planks offered more than enough room to comfortably navigate the staircase.

Every other houseguest had disappeared by now, and every bedroom door on the hall was open. First up was Buck's room, with its empty closet and massive writing desk. Next came the room I used, although it looked like no one had spent much time there. Other than the sheets, which I bunched and swirled during my restless night, nothing else looked used.

I wished I could have spent more time in the beautiful room, because an antique bookcase held a week's worth of paperbacks, and an enormous picture window offered ample reading light. The perfect place to unwind after a hectic weekend, like the one we'd just gone through.

I forced myself to continue walking. After a moment, I made it to Jamie's room, which sat at the very end of the hall. Like before, the drawers of the dresser were all askew, and fat pillows tumbled from the bed to the floor.

I understood why Nelle had called this the "blue room," though, because heavy velvet curtains as blue as the sky lined the windows, with porcelain tiebacks that pulled the fabric away from the glass.

The room held several pieces of heavy furniture, including the four-poster bed, a captain's chair, and an antique writing desk, which was wedged under a large window. The desktop lay bare, except for a few pieces of writing paper. I meandered over to the papers and gazed at the first one on the stack. It looked like an ordinary grocery list, with most of the items crossed out. Alongside everyday items like deodorant and mouthwash, someone had written "apple" and "matches" to end the list.

"Say, Lance?"

He stopped whatever he was doing and crossed the room to the desk. "Yeah?"

"What do you think of this?" I pointed at the list, which someone had written in both blue and black ink.

"Looks to me like Mr. Lee picked up a few things before he got here." Lance reached behind his back and withdrew a pair of latex gloves from his pocket. Ever the Boy Scout, he seemed to stash everything inside those pockets but the kitchen sink. "I'll take this down to the lab and have it dusted for fingerprints."

"Just a second." I lightly stilled his hand. "I understand why he'd want matches. He couldn't very well offer Wesley one of his doctored cigarettes without also offering him a match. But why would he need an apple?"

Lance didn't hesitate. "People put loose tobacco on a slice of apple to keep it from drying out. My grandfather used to do that. Jamie probably knew it'd take him some time to grind up the poison, and he didn't want the cigarette to fall apart when he was done. That's my guess, anyway."

"No wonder you're a detective. I never would've thought of that."

Lance deftly scooped up the list and placed it in the bag. "That guy really knew what he was doing."

"Or maybe Lorelei did. She might've been the one to prepare the poison, for all we know."

"You're right. See, now you're thinking like a detective: look at all the possibilities. Don't sell yourself short, Missy."

I chuckled. "Thanks, but I think I'll stick to making hats. Your job sounds interesting, but I could never do what you do. I don't have the heart to chase down criminals, or the stomach for it."

"That's only one part of the job. Anyway, I'm going to head into the bathroom next. He might've left something in there by accident."

While Lance left to scope out the bathroom, I studied the sheet of paper that remained on the desk. Unlike the shopping list, it hadn't been used. I began to turn away, when the sun suddenly popped out from behind a cloud and bathed the desktop in sunlight.

Why, the other sheet wasn't blank at all! Tiny indentations formed words where someone had written something on a sheet placed over this one. Did Jamie write another note, and not realize his handwriting would appear on the bottom sheet, too?

Since Lance was busy searching the bathroom, I bent lower to examine the paper. It was short—only a sentence long—but succinct:

One seed = .1 milligram. Fatal at 10 milligrams.

Gracious light! It was the recipe for making thorn apple lethal! The author knew exactly how many seeds would kill Wesley. But who? Was Jamie telling the truth when he said he only wanted to make Wesley sick, or did he mean to kill him all along? Did Lorelei join him in this room, and was it her handwriting on the bottom sheet?

"Lance!"

Once more, something rustled as Lance dashed out of the bathroom and into the bedroom.

"What's up?"

I silently pointed to the piece of paper. But just when he was about to examine it, a cloud moved across the sky and darkened the bedroom.

"I don't see anything," he said.

"Wait a minute. You will."

We both waited for the cloud to pass, and when it did, warm sunlight once more bathed the desk in light.

"Huh," he said. "What do you know."

"The sun happened to hit it just right. Someone wrote the directions for making thorn apple toxic. Apparently, the killer needed at least a hundred seeds."

Out came another plastic bag from Lance's pocket.

"How deep are those pockets?" I couldn't help but smile, since his khakis reminded me of all the times I'd watched clowns perform at Ringling

Bros. and Barnum & Bailey Circus. Invariably, a portly clown would pull a menagerie of items from his pants, including a plastic bouquet of flowers and a full bottle of seltzer water. Somehow, the pockets never seemed to empty.

"Don't worry about my pockets. I've learned what I need—and what I don't—over the years. These bags can hold evidence, or work as a glove, or even carry liquids. Leave me and my pants out of this."

"Okay. No need to be defensive. Can't a girl be curious?"

He ignored that last remark. "It looks like we're done here." He stashed the evidence bag away. "I need to head over to the station and have a little chat with our suspects."

"I'd love to join you, but if I don't go back to my studio now, I have a sneaking suspicion my assistant will lock herself in the bathroom. You know, to escape the thundering hordes of brides."

"I get it. Thanks again for helping me out. I'll call you later."

"But not too late, okay?" I yawned loudly, the exhaustion hitting me full-force. "I'm planning to hit the hay as soon as I can. What could possibly happen now?"

Chapter 22

A few minutes later, I pulled away from Honeycutt Hall and drove down the road to Bleu Bayou. Nothing accompanied me but a giant cup of Community Coffee and the latest Harry Connick, Jr., CD.

The noon sun hung directly overhead, and heat seeped through the windshield. I turned the AC to high as I studied the landscape. The first thing I came across was a petroleum plant, with the requisite smokestack that belched white steam into the sky, like a chimney on a locomotive.

Next up was a sugarcane field, with plants that reached about five feet high. Those stalks would double in height by the time fall rolled around and farmers harvested them, but today they barely reached my chin.

Thank goodness for Harry and his energetic crooning, because my head grew heavy as I cruised into the parking lot of the Factory, which was a former hot-sauce plant turned shopping center.

Once upon a time, the building in front of me provided the entire country with hot sauce, and remnants of its former life remained. A glass atrium placed between two of the wings used to hold manufacturing equipment, while the interior artwork came from produce crates that shipped chili peppers and whatnot. Even the rain barrels in the parking lot had a purpose, since they had held ingredients like cayenne pepper and salt.

I pulled up in front of my shop, relieved to find the parking lot half-empty. Other than my Volkswagen, Ringo, the only other cars I spied were Beatrice's bubblegum-pink Ford and a few white delivery vans. She'd sounded so frantic earlier, but maybe this was the lull between storms.

I threw open the car door and stepped onto the asphalt. Although it had to be ninety degrees outside, the heat was the least of my worries. I hadn't peered into a mirror all morning, and I could only imagine how frightful

I looked. Usually, my shoulder-length hair cooperated, thanks to the help of a straightening iron, but all I'd had this morning was a plastic comb and some tap water to tame it. Neglect plus humidity would equal some crazy curls, and one brushed my cheek as I ambled over to the store's French doors.

Funny, but someone had left the doors ajar. Normally, we slammed the doors shut to lock the air-conditioning inside and keep the sticky heat outside. I tapped the door open and tentatively stepped onto the welcome mat inside the shop.

"Hello?" For some reason, every light was off, and what little light remained came from the display window by my cash register. "Anyone home?"

At that moment, the lights flicked on and a chorus of voices greeted me. "Surprise!"

It was quite a gathering. Someone had pulled a display table to the back of the room and then dressed it with fine linens and delicate bone china. A sweating champagne bucket stood at attention nearby. Best of all, my sweet fiancé sat at one of the place settings, with another reserved for me.

In addition to Bo, I spied Beatrice, my intrepid assistant, and Odilia LaPorte, the matriarch of Miss Odilia's Southern Eatery.

"Did we surprise you?" Ambrose gazed at me hopefully. Today he wore my favorite azure polo, which played up his Tiffany-blue eyes, and he'd slicked his hair back with mousse.

Talk about a sight for sore eyes.

"Did you ever!" I hurried over to him and the others, momentarily forgetting my exhaustion. "To what do I owe the pleasure?"

"To the weekend you've had." He gestured over his shoulder, to a serving cart I hadn't noticed before. It held silver chafing dishes stuffed with fried chicken and fluffy butter biscuits—Odilia's specialties. No doubt the fare came straight from the kitchen of her restaurant.

I reached for a biscuit without thinking.

"Careful," she said. "They're hot. Don't want to burn yourself."

I ignored the warning and took a hearty bite. Say what you would about the calorie count, but nothing could appease an empty stomach like one of Miss Odilia's biscuits.

"Mm, hmm." I hastily swallowed my mouthful. "That's worth burning my tongue for."

"I almost forgot something." Beatrice hustled away from the table, and then she returned a moment later. "Look! Your veil turned out perfect. You can't even see the stain."

She held out the bridal veil, which was fashioned from very delicate, and very expensive, antique Alençon lace. The lace flowed across the table and pooled in my lap.

"You're right." I held the biscuit at arms' length so it wouldn't touch the veil as I studied the lace. The entire veil was eggshell white, softly faded with age, and I'd lined the scalloped edges with hundreds of tiny seed pearls that sparkled just so in the light. A pattern embroidered in the center evoked a large garden rose in full bloom.

"Whoa." Ambrose leaned away from the table. "Isn't it bad luck for the groom to see that stuff before the wedding?"

"We'll make an exception this time." I winked at Beatrice, and she whisked the veil away from me. "Okay, that's one problem solved. At last count, we had at least two more, and there are only a few weeks to go until the wedding."

The thought made me cringe, even with the wonderful tableau in front of me. I had labored under a cloud of worry all weekend. Not just about the murder, which was horrible enough, but about all the things that had gone wrong with the wedding plans.

"Well, it looks like your veil turned out fine." Ambrose held three fingers in the air as he counted down his points. "That's one problem solved. Then I already told you the photographer agreed to shoot our pictures. That's number two."

I felt my shoulders untense, ever so slightly. "You're right. But we still don't have a place to hold it, and we *can't* use our backyard."

"Why not?" His smile was playful. "I can even move the barbecue grill behind the garage, if you ask me nicely."

"Very funny. The way I figure it, we've got two hundred guests coming, and nowhere to put them."

"Really?" Odilia hadn't spoken for a while, and I almost forgot she was there. "Are you sure about that? Have you thought about using my restaurant?"

My mind reeled. I hadn't thought about it. Which was ridiculous, because her restaurant would be a perfect site. A wonderful solution. A...

"Wait a minute." When reality hit, it hit hard. "We're about talking about a Saturday night, Odilia. Where you serve, what, about five hundred dinners? Plus, all that takeout. I couldn't possibly ask you to give up that kind of revenue."

"Pshaw," she said. "What's a little lost revenue between friends? You know, you could always hold the ceremony in the main dining room, and then we could flip it for the reception. Of course, there might be some downtime between the two. Hadn't really thought about that."

We all fell silent, until Ambrose snapped his fingers. "Wait a second! What about using the Rising Tide Baptist Church? You know, the place where we held that fashion show a few years ago."

My jaw fell open. I hadn't thought about that little country church in ages. While Ambrose and I attended a much larger church about a half hour away, the country chapel was right next door, in Riversbend.

I automatically beamed. "Of course! I'm surprised we didn't think of that sooner."

A few years ago, when I first opened Crowning Glory, I met Ambrose at his studio next door, and we hit it off right away. We both worked at a wedding at a place called Morningside, where I happened to stumble upon a quaint country church on one of my walks.

It turned out the church needed help with a fundraiser, so I volunteered to help them stage a fashion show. Ever since then, the church had held a soft spot in my heart.

Unfortunately, reality returned much too soon. "But the chapel is really tiny. I seem to recall it only holds about fifty people."

"That's true." Ambrose played with a napkin ring. "It'd be much too tight for our crew. Unless—"

We both reached the same conclusion at the same time.

"The social hall!"

We'd staged the fashion show in a large social hall located at the back of the church's property. The room could easily hold five hundred people, or twice as many as we needed room for. It was a blank canvas, perfect for adding special touches, like twinkling lights, fabric walls, and gorgeous topiary sculptures, courtesy of my favorite landscaper, Darryl.

"That's a wonderful plan," Odilia agreed. "Afterward, you can come back to my restaurant and have the reception in the main dining room."

Beatrice decided to get in on the action, and she leaned forward excitedly. "You can even use my Ford truck as your getaway car."

The thought of rumbling away from my wedding in a vintage bubblegum-pink Ford brought a smile to my face.

"Ambrose?" While I wanted more than anything to say yes to all the excited plans, I had no idea what he thought of them.

"Are you kidding?" He reached for the champagne bottle in response. "I'm in."

"Great. I'll contact them tomorrow. One last thing." I cut my gaze to Beatrice. "What was all this talk about a crazy day at the shop yesterday? Did you just say that to lure me in today?"

"Maybe." She toyed with the words. "Or maybe I really needed you, but I handled everything myself. In which case, you're welcome."

Bo winked at her, which gave me my answer.

"Why, Beatrice Rushing. You lied! You said the studio was chockablock with customers and you needed me to get back here, pronto."

"And it worked perfectly, didn't it?"

Leave it to Beatrice to show no shame when it came to fooling me. I still intended to stuff a nice, fat bonus into her next paycheck, but now I thought about adding a whoopee cushion or something equally silly to even the score.

"I've said it before, and I'll say it again." Bo interrupted our make-believe spat by dredging the champagne bottle from the icy water. "I'd marry you in a bowling alley, Missy DuBois."

Sweet of him to say that. And thank goodness it wouldn't come to that.

Chapter 23

Once Ambrose and I polished off the dinner provided by Odilia, it was time to go home. To the sweet little cottage on the outskirts of town, where nothing exciting ever happened, which was just the way I liked it.

I rode with Ambrose in his car, since we could always return to the Factory to pick up my Volkswagen later. We pulled onto Highway 18, prepared to leave Bleu Bayou, when I thought of something.

"You know, I'm glad we'll be home soon. I have a feeling Stormie is going to lead off the newscast this evening."

He glanced at me warily. "What's the deal with you two? I thought you hated her."

"Hate? That's much too strong a word. We have our differences, that's all."

"Seems to me, your 'differences' happen every other day."

I playfully swatted his arm as our drive continued. Before long, we pulled up to the "rent house," and Ambrose extinguished the engine.

Unlike Honeycutt Hall, the tiny cottage in front of us could fit in the palm of a giant's hand. Early on, I planted a wisteria bush over an arched trellis, and the blossoms dipped over a brick path that led to the front door. Nothing about the house said "grand." Not the crooked shutters or the overgrown wisteria or a garden gnome that waited for us near the front door.

I paused to pat the gnome for good luck—it was a silly tradition we started a few years ago—and ambled into the living room. Now I was both sleepy and full, which meant I'd barely crossed the threshold before I flopped onto the sofa.

"Ambrose? Could you please be a dear and bring me the remote?"

He pretended to bow as he scooped it off the table. "As you wish, m'lady."

I caught the remote when he tossed it to me, and then I automatically turned to KATC. Channel 11 came through loud and clear on our set, since the signal originated in Baton Rouge, which couldn't be said for some of the other channels. The reception for phones and our television was iffy, at best, which only added to the house's charm, or so we told ourselves.

Ambrose joined me on the couch, and he draped his arm across my shoulders. To feel him so close to me was heavenly, and I sighed deeply as I laid my head on his shoulder.

"Shhh," he teased. "The news is starting."

Right there, on the screen in front of us, appeared Stormie, in all her technicolor glory. She still wore the crimson jacket from earlier, only she'd added some chunky gold earrings and a matching necklace to the mix.

"Honestly, you'd think they'd hire a professional makeup person for her," I whispered.

"What? And spoil the fun for the rest of us?"

Like always, Stormie looked like she'd applied her makeup with a trowel, and a thick line appeared where the foundation ended at her chin. She also wore false eyelashes again, not to mention about a gallon of eyeliner. Too bad she didn't know the art of subtlety, because she was a pretty woman under all that paint.

"As many of our viewers know, the family of Wesley Carmichael finally got a break in the case today." She looked straight into the camera.

So far, so good. She didn't seem nervous about appearing in the studio, since she normally reported her stories from the field. Apparently, this was the "big break" she'd been hoping for, and the reason she hung around Honeycutt Hall all weekend.

"I had a chance to speak with the lieutenant in charge of the case," she continued, "a Detective Lance LaPorte with the Bleu Bayou Police Department."

She pointed to the screen behind her, where Lance's face suddenly appeared on footage shot earlier by her cameraman. The video showed Lance and Stormie standing in the pull-through drive in front of the mansion, and Lance looked twice as nervous as Stormie did.

"Detective, what can you tell us about the latest development in the case?" she asked.

I knew Lance well enough to know when he was uncomfortable, and his gaze flickered back and forth across the screen. It was his patented "I'd rather be anywhere else than here" look, which I'd seen countless times over the years.

"We apprehended two suspects in this case. Apparently, the victim was poisoned overnight on Friday, and the suspects are well known to the Carmichaels."

"Well known?" Ambrose was incredulous. "I'd say they're well known. Considering one of them almost married their son."

"Shhh." I playfully poked him in the ribs. "Let her talk."

"I understand the defendants decided to plead guilty," she continued. "What does that mean for the case?"

"Anytime suspects plead guilty, it means they're waiving their right to a jury trial. In this case, they must've been swayed by the amount of evidence stacked against them."

"That's fascinating." Stormie leaned closer to Lance, as if they were best friends or something.

"She doesn't even know him, Ambrose," I said. "Look at her! She's acting like they're best friends."

Ambrose shrugged. "She's okay. Are you sure you're not jealous?"

"Go on." I swatted his arm again. "Jealous of Stormie? Ha! That's a laugh."

Fortunately, the interview continued, so I didn't have to dwell on it. It wasn't that I envied Stormie, but she always seemed to get what she wanted. Lead story on the nightly news? Check. Exclusive interview with a detective on the case? Check. Whereas I felt like I was swimming upstream most of time, trying to keep my small business afloat and my personal life on track, Stormie made everything look so easy. Almost too easy.

"I understand you were the one who solved this case," Stormie said on the video. "Can you tell our viewers what tipped you off?"

"Actually…" Here, Lance faltered, as if he couldn't quite decide how to phrase his next thought. "That's not entirely true. I had help."

"Help?" Stormie frowned, clearly not expecting that answer. "But I thought you were the lead detective on the case."

"I am, but I have a very special friend who helped me crack it. I'd like to thank Missy DuBois for her assistance in solving the murder. I couldn't have done it without her."

"Awww." I leaned my head back on Ambrose's shoulder as I listened to the newscast. "How nice of him to say that."

Stormie sniffed at the comment, though. "Well, that may be, but I understand you were the one who took the suspects into custody. Anyway, now that guilty pleas have been entered, we'll see how the judge reacts when it comes time to sentence them."

With that, the video ended and the camera cut back to Stormie in the studio. She seemed pleased with her report, because she grinned from ear to ear. Yep, it seemed awfully easy for Stormie to get everything she ever wanted. If only life happened that way for the rest of us.

"Thank you for that report, Stormie," the anchor told her. "Now I understand you have some news for our viewers."

"I do." She tugged at the bottom of her jacket, which barely closed over her bulging stomach. "Today is my last day at the station. I've decided to leave for 'personal reasons.'" She flicked two fingers up and down to indicate air quotes around the phrase.

"Good luck with the newborn." The anchor, on the other hand, obviously hadn't been coached by a human resources rep on what to say, because he felt no need to hide the truth. "We've very excited for you. Up next, a look at the weather as we enter our workweek."

I turned to Ambrose on the couch, incredulous. "I don't believe it. Stormie just gave up her perfect career for her family?"

It seemed completely out of character, and it turned my impression of her on its head. I always assumed Stormie cared more about herself more than anyone else.

"Hey," Ambrose said. "People change. Isn't that what keeps life interesting?"

"You're right, of course." I made a mental note to call Stormie tomorrow and congratulate her. Not to mention, to get ahold of Lance so I could thank him for including me in his statement. "I guess it wouldn't hurt if I reached out to her. You know, to smooth things over."

"No, it wouldn't hurt. But first, you need to get some rest. You've had a big weekend. Probably the biggest one yet."

"And thank goodness it's over." My eyes slowly drooped closed. "Not a moment too soon."

Chapter 24

The morning of August 10, the day of my wedding, I awoke to thunderclouds hovering behind the bedroom window. The clouds hung low in the sky and turned everything gunmetal gray. "Butter my biscuits!"

I immediately hopped out of bed and threw on a bathrobe. Out of all the days for it to rain, why did it have to be today?

My eyes misted as I headed to the kitchen, even though I didn't need more water in my life. How could I forget the way Lorelei panicked when a thundershower threatened *her* wedding weekend? Even though a rainstorm turned out to be the least of her worries, I remembered feeling sorry for her and throwing her one of my patented "bless your hearts."

Now *I* was the one people would feel sorry for, and I was the one they'd lob that little bon mot at.

I rounded the corner into the kitchen, where I automatically checked a clock built into the microwave. The hands stood at nine and twelve. Thankfully, Beatrice would be here in about an hour, since I'd promised to do her hair and makeup for the wedding, and she'd promised to do the same for me. Beatrice would know how to make me feel better.

One glance through the kitchen window, though, and I realized some of our plans would have to change. Instead of enjoying mimosas in the backyard, for example, we might have to settle for champagne in the kitchen. And instead of picking roses from my garden for the head table? I'd have to call Darryl and ask him to supply yet one more bouquet.

Luckily, Ambrose wasn't here to see me, since I didn't want to hear the advice he'd no doubt offer. For some reason, he thought anytime I complained about something, like the weather, it meant I wanted him to fix it. More often than not, though, I only wanted a sounding board, and I wasn't asking for a solution.

Since he couldn't do anything about the rain, he'd probably say something only a man would appreciate, such as, "Bet you nobody will even notice." Which made no sense, because I obviously noticed. Not to mention the wedding photographer would, since she'd have to change her plans and take all of the pictures indoors now.

Being a superstitious sort, Ambrose had decided to spend the night with his best man, Hollis. Hollis owned an alligator farm nearby, and he practically grew up in Ambrose's shadow.

Sadly, Hollis lost his grandmother Ruby last fall, who was the closest thing he'd had to a parent. Ever since that time, Ambrose had taken him under his wing, and now Hollis and he were inseparable. When Ambrose asked Hollis to be his best man at the wedding, I thought the boy would melt into a puddle of happiness.

Before I got too far into the kitchen, the telephone next to the stove rang. I reached for it cautiously, since I had no idea who'd be calling me this morning.

"Good morning!"

It sounded like Bettina LeBlanc, the lady who owned Pink Cake Boxes. Bettina was known far and wide for creating the most amazing cakes and pies, and her waiting list during the wedding season ballooned to three months or more. Since she was a personal friend of mind, though—not to mention my neighbor at the Factory—she'd agreed to bake my cake with only a month's notice.

"Is that you, Bettina? Can you believe it's raining? Raining!"

"Now, Missy." Sure enough, I'd recognize her tone anywhere. Bettina and I had worked on many weddings together, and she always managed to stay cool, calm, and collected.

"You know what they say," she continued. "It's—"

"Don't say it! Don't you dare tell me it's good luck when it rains on your wedding day! We both know that's not true."

"Oohhh…should I come over? You sound like you're about to jump out a window."

"All my windows are on the first floor." Despite everything, I felt a grin coming on. "I can't exactly jump off a one-story building."

"Good. No need to. Not when you hear what I have planned."

My curiosity piqued, I momentarily forgot about the weather long enough to pull out a barstool by the counter and take a seat. "Fire away. I need some good news this morning."

"Well, I was just about to put the finishing touches on your cake. But then, I had this brilliant idea. I know we talked about decorating the top with orchids, but how about if I use a lady's hat instead?"

Again, I smiled, despite myself. "That's an awesome idea! I absolutely love it. You can pull one of the hats out of the shop. Pick any one you think will work."

Being neighbors at the Factory, I kept a key to Bettina's studio, and she kept one to mine. That was one of the best things about living in a small town like Bleu Bayou. Everyone watched out for everyone else. Since we all minded each other's property, crime stayed at a minimum. Except, of course, for the murders that happened to pop up every now and again. Add those into the total, and our small town's crime stats went through the roof.

"Well, I'd better dash," she said. "I have another surprise for you, but I don't want to tip my hand."

"Wait a min—"

She clicked off the line before I could finish. Another surprise? Whatever could she mean? We'd discussed the cake in detail just this past week. Thank goodness she was a true professional and I trusted her judgment, since I pretty much gave her carte blanche to create a cake for the ceremony. Time would tell whether that was a wise decision.

I spent the next hour slowly waking up with a cup of Community Coffee in one hand, and the latest issue of the *Bleu Bayou Impartial Reporter* in the other. By now, everyone knew about the arrests of Lorelei and Jamie, but the paper continued to provide updates as the case moved through the St. James Parish Criminal Court.

It turned out both of them changed their pleas to "not guilty" at their arraignments, so they'd be eligible for jury trials. The first step was to hold preliminary hearings, where Lance and his team provided enough evidence to a judge to bring the cases to trial.

The next step involved sitting two separate grand juries to hear the charges. Based on the juries' decisions, the duo would be indicted for their crimes, or not. Not surprisingly, defense attorneys had a heck of a time finding twenty-three people for each jury who didn't know the Carmichaels, the Honeycutts, or Jamie Lee's family.

So the defense attorneys filed motions to change the venue to a larger city, like New Orleans or Baton Rouge, but there was no telling whether that would happen at this point.

I thought about the case, and everyone involved in it, until a strike of lightning jolted my attention back to the kitchen. Rain began to fall, softly at first, and then with a thunderous clap that almost obscured the sound of my ringing doorbell. *Almost.*

I yelped and slid off the barstool. By the time I reached the front door, Beatrice was already entering the room.

"Hello, hello," she said, brightly.

"Hey."

"You don't sound like someone who's getting married today."

"Do you blame me? Look outside."

"What's a little rain on a day like today? Look at it this way, your ceremony's inside and so is your reception. What more do you want?"

"How about a dry spell between the hours of four and midnight?" I was only half-joking, but she laughed along with me anyway.

"You might just get it. In the meantime, I brought enough Saran Wrap to cover you up like a mummy when you have to go from the church to the reception."

"I knew there was a reason why I loved you so much."

We opened a bottle of Dom right then and there, and then she set to work doing my hair and makeup. By the time she finished, a lovely updo swept my auburn hair to one side, and we'd polished off an entire bottle of Dom. Then we gossiped about this, that, and the other thing while I returned the favor and fixed her hair and makeup.

Once finished, we decided we'd carry my dress to the church, since we didn't want to risk muddying the hem. I'd chosen a lovely A-line dress I found at a local resale shop. The way I figured it, I had more than enough expenses at Crowning Glory, not to mention all the bills that would come due after the wedding, so a brand-new dress was out of the question.

And although the dress wasn't new, it was pretty, with an illusion neckline and a frothy tulle skirt that swirled around my ankles when I tried it on. Best of all, the color was ivory, instead of white, so the antique lace veil would match the eggshell fabric.

Fortunately, the rain slackened slightly—although it didn't stop altogether—by the time we wrapped everything up at the house. I headed to the coat closet to retrieve the dress, and that was when the telephone stopped me short.

"Sassafrass!" I said. "I'll never make it to the church at this rate!"

"Leave it." Beatrice reached for the doorknob with her free hand, since she carried my veil and shoes with her other one. "You can't be late today."

My insatiable curiously got the best of me, though, like it always did, and I lunged for the phone before the ringing subsided. "Hello?"

A chuckle sounded. "Aren't you supposed to be at the church soon, Mrs. Jackson?"

"Ambrose! I thought you were worried about bad luck. Doesn't talking with your bride right before the ceremony count?"

While I liked to tease my fiancé, the sound of his voice was like music to my ears. It was incredible the way one word from him could change my whole outlook.

"I'm making an exception this time. I need you to get something out of my closet."

Since Ambrose and I shared the cottage, I knew his closet about as well as my own.

"Well, what do you need?"

"It's hanging in a black garment bag, front and center."

"Ambrose! Don't tell me you forgot to bring your tuxedo to the church!" While I tried to sound angry, I wasn't very convincing.

"It's no big deal. But I need you to grab the bag for me."

Before I could ask him any more questions—or chide him about his memory—he hung up.

Beatrice tapped her foot impatiently. "C'mon, Missy. We have to go."

Whether because of the champagne or the sound of my fiancé's voice, my mood had improved considerably. "Hold on. Ambrose forgot something in his closet. It'll only take me a sec."

I left her standing at the door, where a frown darkened her face. To be honest, we still had a few minutes to go before they expected us at the church, and I couldn't very well leave my fiancé twisting in the wind, now could I?

I headed for his room and ducked through the half-closed door. Like me, his room had seen better days, and dirty clothes covered every available surface. He'd made a path to the bed by kicking aside dirty T-shirts and gym shorts, and a pile of used dress shirts puddled near the closet. I understood completely, because neither of us had time to eat or sleep during the wedding season, let alone clean our rooms.

I stepped over the dress shirts when I reached his closet. Just like he promised, the garment bag hung front and center inside, and the sides puffed out curiously. I grabbed the bag, and the thing fell into my arms with a *thunk*. What was inside...half his wardrobe??

I threw the bag on the bed and quickly unzipped it. While I expected to find black tuxedo pants and a stiff white dress shirt, something sparkly winked at me instead. My mouth rounded into an O as I realized what he'd stashed inside the bag.

It was a gown: a frothy confection of tulle, glass crystals, and lovingly applied seed pearls. Cautiously, I reached for the dress and gently dislodged it from the hanger.

"What the—"

"Missy?"

I turned to see Beatrice standing in the doorway, her expression curious.

"Look, Bea!"

I swept the dress from the bag and held it up. We both gasped at the same time when we saw the beautifully embellished silk bodice, which was nipped at the waist, the cascade of seed pearls, which tumbled down the tulle skirt, and the delicate scalloped edges lined with genuine Swarovski crystals.

"He didn't!" she gasped.

"He did." I moved over to a full-length mirror Ambrose kept on the back of his door. While Beatrice scooted out of the way, I clasped the dress in front of me, too stunned for words.

It was, without a doubt, the most beautiful dress I'd ever seen.

"You have to try it on," Beatrice said. "Now!"

I slipped out of my sundress and kicked it aside. Then I carefully stepped through the folds of fabric. Once I stepped through the waistband and shimmied into the bodice, which featured a sweetheart neckline and cap sleeves, I turned to let Beatrice button up the back. More than two dozen covered buttons cinched the lace together, and the look on her face when she finished fastening them told me everything I needed to know.

"It's beautiful, isn't it?" I fluffed out the dress with my palms, and then I watched it softly billow back into place in the mirror.

"Missy, you look like a dream." She cautiously reached out to touch the dress, the tulle separated from the silk bodice by a rhinestone belt. Like me, she couldn't wait to feel the exquisite texture of the fabric. Between the sprinkle of seed pearls and the glimmering rhinestone belt, it all sparkled like sunlight.

"It's official," I said, once I took it all in. "I have the best fiancé ever."

"And you can't even see the back. It's beautiful." Beatrice sounded flabbergasted. "Do you know how long it must've taken him just to attach the buttons?"

"Trust me, I know. Can I have my phone, please?"

While Beatrice left to grab my cell, I took one last look at Ambrose's gift. The waist...the length...the bodice. Everything fit to a T. Knowing Ambrose, he'd kidnapped some of the dresses from my closet to get the dimensions just right. If I had any reservations about the ceremony today—rain and all—they disappeared in a swirl of off-white tulle and sparkly silk.

Beatrice returned with the cell a moment later.

"Here...could you please hold this?" I carefully passed her the dress while I dialed Ambrose's number.

After three rings, the recorded message clicked on.

"You've reached Ambrose's Allure Couture. I'll call you back—"

I hung up the phone, disappointed. "Guess I'll have to thank him at the church. It's now or never."

Beatrice and I left the cottage soon afterward, the voluminous ballgown tucked back into the garment bag for safekeeping. Although the clouds managed to hold back the worst of the rain, a soft shower fell all around us. Meanwhile, Beatrice juggled my shoes, accessories, and makeup bag in her arms as she steered us toward her classic Ford truck.

I was about to toss my duffel bag into the truck bed when I noticed something else.

"Beatrice? What the heck?"

Someone had attached a hand-painted sign to the pickup's tailgate that read His & Hers. Pink streamers trailed from the sign to the ground, and each one held an empty can of Parish Brewing Pale Ale, which was Ambrose's favorite beverage. Mardi Gras beads covered every leftover inch on the sign.

"That's Uncle Hank's handiwork." She winked.

I'd grown close to Hank Dupre, Beatrice's uncle, over the years, and I considered him my uncle by now. Hank was the one who purchased the old Sweetwater mansion next door, even after Ambrose and I made a gruesome discovery in an outbuilding, and it was Hank who loaned me a pirogue anytime I needed to navigate the Atchafalaya River. Leave it to him to add a touch of whimsy to our ceremony, Cajun style.

Beatrice and I hopped into the truck and thumped along the road until we reached the Rising Tide Baptist Church. Thankfully, traffic was light, since few people traversed the roads on a Saturday, especially so near the dinner hour. By the time we arrived at the church, the parking lot was half full, and I immediately recognized several cars.

Over there, by the back door to the sanctuary, sat Ambrose's gleaming Audi Quattro. The car had taken us on many interesting adventures, including a fast getaway from a voodoo ceremony, of all things, and a memorable drive to Commander's Palace in New Orleans.

Next to the Audi was Grady Sebastian's hulking Ford Mustang. The shiny red muscle car was as brash and brawny as its owner. Although it seemed like a century ago now, I once went out with Grady, back when I thought Ambrose and I might be on the skids. My, how times had changed.

Finally, I noticed Lance's Buick Oldsmobile on the other end of the row. Like always, dirt and grime covered the car, and streaks of dried mud splashed around the wheel wells. Obviously, Lance had yet to visit the Sparkle N' Shine, although I mentioned it all the time.

"Missy?" Beatrice turned to face me once she put the Ford in Park. "Is something wrong? You just sighed."

"No, nothing's wrong." I shook my head to clear it. "You know, when I first moved here, I wondered if I'd made a big mistake. If maybe I should've stayed back in Tennessee when I graduated from college. But you know what? I wouldn't trade this place, or these people, for anything."

She chuckled. "I know just what you mean. I always tell people Bleu Bayou is a real small town but the people have real big hearts." She quickly sobered up. "Are you ready to do this?"

"I am."

We stepped from the car, and I grabbed a duffle bag from the back. Hallelujah, the clouds managed to hold back the rain now, and a few sunbeams even pierced the gloom. I'd been instructed to use the door on the left, which would take me straight to the bride's room…and then the altar.

Chapter 25

Someone waited for me inside the door to the social hall, and I recognized the old man right away.

"Hello again."

It was the deacon who went out of his way to help Ambrose and me during the fashion show a few years back. Like before, he wore a powder-blue suit, and he'd slicked his hair back with about a gallon of Brylcreem. "Hello, Miss DuBois. I'm supposed to escort you to the bride's room."

He automatically reached for my wedding gown, but I drew it close to me. "I'll carry this, if you don't mind."

Instead, he offered me his arm, and we walked through the foyer and into the social hall, which Darryl and his helpers had turned into a veritable wonderland of flowers and lights.

To begin with, my favorite handyman/gardener had installed a blanket of roses where the theater curtain once hung. The blooms' colors gradually blurred from white on one end to fuchsia on the other, with stops at cherry blossom, blush, and raspberry in between.

Then Darryl created miniature topiaries for each table, the three tiers strung with dozens of tiny lights that extended from their bases to their tippy-tops. To complement the garden theme, he draped each place setting with a spray of pink wisteria.

I found Darryl by the side of the social hall, leaning over a centerpiece that wasn't up to snuff.

"There you are!" I quickly gave him a big hug.

Although Darryl tried to come across as gruff on the outside, I suspected marshmallow fluff filled his insides.

"Thank you so much for the beautiful decorations! You've outdone yourself."

His cheeks instantly turned about as red as the last color on the curtain of roses.

"'Tweren't nuthin'." He bashfully stared at the ground while he spoke, and I imagined he tried to grind his toe into the floor, although I couldn't see it.

"You're wrong about that. Everyone will feel like they're sitting in a garden. A magical garden. Thank you."

"Aw, go on." He nodded at the watch on his wrist. "I mean it. You need to go. It's almost five."

I yelped and turned away from him. Beatrice already stood on the other side of the room, and she was about to disappear through a doorway to the bride's suite. Meanwhile, my elderly escort waited for me by a huge flower urn busting with Stargazer lilies.

"Thanks again!" I yelled, as I dashed away.

In my haste, I nearly collided with a round table by the exit. Luckily, I skidded to a stop just in time, and the dress swooshed against the table's edge. On it, Bettina had balanced a perfect reproduction of my wedding cake, only she'd constructed this one of Styrofoam and chicken wire instead of flour and egg whites. The faux cake soared four feet tall and it held five different layers of beautiful designs. She must've constructed the model to help her plan the final product, or she wanted to create a "dummy cake" to display in her bakery later.

One time, Bettina explained how and why she created models of her elaborate cake designs. Every time clients stepped into her bakery at the Factory, they invariably drifted over to a gleaming display case, and she wanted the products inside to remain fresh for months, if not years.

These samples had to withstand both changes in the temperature and the invariable ravages of time. Instead of spongy cake under the frosting, Bettina placed blocks of Styrofoam, which she first cut into specific shapes. Then she iced the blocks using a modified recipe for the frosting, or even spackle, if she planned to keep the dummy cake for several years.

Finally, she stayed away from bright colors for the frosting, which would fade under the fluorescent lights, and stuck to neutrals like beige or cream.

Amazing how many details Bettina had taught me about cake making since she introduced herself as a new tenant in the Factory way back in 2016.

"It's so beautiful!" I sputtered.

Whatever doubts I'd had about a cake for the reception instantly evaporated. Bettina had outdone herself, and I'd seen some pretty incredible cakes from her in the past.

For this one, she'd separated the two sides with black and white "dummy" frosting. Or, to be more accurate, with colors to represent vanilla and chocolate frosting. Instead of icing a straight line down the middle to separate the two sides, she gently curved a ribbon of silver fondant between them.

On one side—the bride's—she iced fake vanilla frosting into edible roses that stairstepped down the cake. Somehow, she managed to trim the bottom layer with delicate white lace frosting, which looked opaque against the cake. As the pièce de résistance, she balanced a woman's fascinator at the very top, with a delicate net veil that mirrored the cake's border.

For the groom's side, she repeated the lace border, but with chocolate "frosting." She also added some brown leaves to give it a more masculine touch than the bride's roses. Finally, she placed a top hat on the groom's side, which she tilted to one side.

Even the model looked far too pretty to eat. I made a mental note to give the photographer plenty of time to capture shots of Bettina's creation before we served it to our guests, so we could preserve it for all time.

I finally tore myself away from Bettina's model, and then I continued to the bride's suite. Once Beatrice had helped me into my gown, the photographer took a few pictures, with just the two of us, and then I tried to remain calm as I waited for Lance to come and get me.

Being an orphan, and an only child at that, I didn't have an immediate family member to walk me down the aisle. What I did have was a best friend in Lance, and I didn't want anyone but him beside me when I made the trek to the altar.

He arrived a few minutes later, wearing his policeman dress blues. With a starched shirt trimmed with gold epaulets and tons of braid, he looked especially regal—not to mention highly uncomfortable.

I straightened his tie a smidge. "You clean up well, but I bet you'd rather be in your khakis, right?"

"Don't you know it. These pants don't have any pockets to speak of."

He playfully patted his pants' pockets, which lay flat against his legs. "By the way…you clean up well, too. You look like a Disney princess."

He must've misread the look on my face, because he immediately added, "And that's a good thing. Like you're going to a ball or something."

"Or something." I smiled broadly. "My new husband designed it."

"I would've put my money on a cast of cartoon mice and a fairy godmother. Are you ready for this?"

"Definitely."

I threaded my arm through his, and we left the bride's room. A low murmur greeted us as we stepped into the church's foyer, behind the closed doors of the sanctuary. Although I had no idea how many people waited for us on the other side, I guessed the crowd to be about two hundred or so. Thankfully, my wonderful maid of honor had handled the guest list, which freed me up to worry about the music, menu, and whatnot.

Beatrice took her place at the front of our little procession, and the doors whisked open. Everything blurred in my periphery as Lance and I marched down the aisle. Every once in a while, a face beamed back at me that I couldn't help but notice.

I first noticed Ivy Solomon, a longtime friend who lived in Baton Rouge. Somehow, Ivy managed to keep her wits about her, even after several tragedies upended her world. I wasn't surprised to see Ivy wearing a classic St. John suit and one of my fascinators, since she possessed a gracious style and a keen sense of loyalty.

A few rows up, I spotted Stormie Lanai, who teetered uncertainly on her heels, now that she was halfway through the pregnancy. Although Stormie and I shared a rocky past, we put all that behind us once and for all a few weeks ago. I told her how much I admired her for putting her family first, and she admitted she envied me because of my studio. In the end, we were more alike than different, so we agreed to let bygones be bygones.

Finally, I noticed Waunzy Boudin, who sat in the second row. Waunzy chaired the Bleu Bayou Historical Society, and she knew the antebellum homes around here like the back of her hand. Waunzy grinned at me as I passed, her face collapsing into a patchwork of wrinkles under the brim of her yellow sunbonnet.

At last I reached the altar, where my handsome groom stood waiting.

"Funny to see you here," he whispered, as Lance slipped my hand into his. Then Lance moved aside, to join the line of groomsmen by the altar.

One look at Ambrose's Tiffany-blue eyes, and I lost all track of time. I only snapped to attention when I felt the pastor's gaze fall on me, and I realized it was my turn to say something.

"You know," I began, "today is the day I've chosen to be your wife. And I will choose you again tomorrow, and all the days after that."

At that point, Ambrose's eyes grew misty and his hand tightened around mine. I opened my mouth again to speak, when something buzzed just over Ambrose's shoulder, near where the groomsmen stood.

In a flash, I recognized the sound, and the look of horror that crossed Lance's face only confirmed it.

Sure enough, he jammed his hand into the pocket of his dress blues and discreetly pulled out his cell. When he stared at it, it was evident that it was police headquarters calling him about yet another murder, because no one ever called Lance with good news. And although this was not the time, nor the place, for things like police business, it couldn't be helped.

He shot me an apologetic glance, but I only shook my head and smiled. While he tiptoed away and disappeared into a side room, I returned my attention to Ambrose.

For once, Lance would have to handle this one on his own. I had more important things to worry about at the moment.

Printed in the United States
by Baker & Taylor Publisher Services